PORT TALBOT PARKWAY

Port Talbot Parkway

LESLEY J LEWIS

6.30am

"What did I do with those teeth?"

"They were just there on the side," came the reply from the bedroom.

"Not those ones, I have those in my mouth already. I meant the ones in the box, the ones we've lost?"

"The ones you've lost, you mean. I hope so, I didn't get up this early for nothing."

"What time is it?"

"Early! Come on, get your trousers on and we'll get going."

"Spoil sport, you always make me wear trousers when we go out, depriving the world of a wonderful sight. Have you got the bag?"

"Yes, come on hurry up. I've got your bag, I've also got your medication for later."

"Has anyone told you how lovely you are?"

8.30am

"Are you ready?"

"Yes, just getting my bits, I'll be there now," came the reply.

Carol was waiting at the open front door with a small bag with everything she needed for the day ahead. She stood waiting to pull it shut. "You said that five minutes ago."

"It was two minutes ago and I'm looking for my keys."

There was a lot of noise from the middle reception room of their terraced house. Janice shoved some essentials into a bag and coat pockets. She was certainly not as organised as her sister Carol, she was more laid back. Some would even say disorganised.

Carol, very much like her dad, was always punctual, ready to leave whenever a time had been agreed. Their late dad liked to be on time, he took pride in being somewhere on time. He took great pleasure if he was early and there-fore, not late. An even greater pleasure was found, if a family day out had been arranged, to beat the traffic, even if that meant leaving hours before any soul had thought of getting out of bed to clog up the roads.

He had worked all his life in the same town as he was born as an accountant in the centre of town, exactly six minutes walk from home. However, he would never take such liberties as starting from the house *exactly* six minutes before he was due to start work, that would be irresponsible. No, he would leave in enough time to pick up his paper from the newsagent on the way, walk the remaining distance to the office, head up stairs to the staff kitchen, make himself a coffee, sit at his desk and mentally review how he was going to tackle the company's client's accounts. He did this for forty years, before collapsing on his way home from the office, with one week to go before retirement. A devastating time for the two sisters, who only lost their mother the previous year, naturally in her sleep.

"I've got them," shouted through Janice.

Both sisters who were unmarried, decided to stay in the family home. Being such an organised and careful planner, their dad had left them in a financially secure position. And both

Carol and Janice decided to give up their jobs to live the *high life.*

Carol and Janice had never been poor and they certainly weren't billionairesses. But they had been left mortgage free, with enough money, split between them, to live off for quite some time, especially if they were careful with it.

Carol was now starting to become a little more impatient, "Come on Janice. Have you got your keys?"

"Yes," came the reply.

"Purse?"

"Yes."

"Flask?"

"Yes."

"Then what are we waiting for? We'll miss the first train if you don't pull your finger out."

Janice came hurrying down the hallway with her jacket on, "Coming, coming, all sorted," she said, putting her woollen bobble hat on, something she would come to regret later.

Bag over her shoulder, patted her pockets just to double-check she had her phone, keys, purse. Yep, all was in order, as she squeezed past Carol out the front door. Carol pulled the knocker and the door rattled shut. She checked it was actually shut by shoving the door and giving the knocker a couple of pulls. Satisfied, she shut the small garden gate fully closed.

Not that it made any difference, it was a gate, but no garden could be attributed to it. All the terraced houses in the street had a four feet bit of land to the front of each house. It was substantial enough to require a three foot brick wall to separate the property from the pathway and from each neighbour. The shutting of the gate was just for completion. To Carol and those like her in the street it just seemed the decent thing to do.

She was on Google Maps one time and discovered Street View, something that was new at the time. She was horrified when she realised the camera car had captured her house with the gate open. What would people think? It took her ages to get over it, until it was explained that Google Maps updates every few years, so she had some hope of rectifying the issue.

As they were just to walk down the street to go to the station she caught sight of the window cleaner. She would have to pay him later, she didn't have the time for small talk just now. The first train was due. She knew if she got caught, she'd be chatting with him for a full fifteen minutes. She wouldn't have usually minded, but he spent most of the time complaining about the restricted parking in the streets and the traffic wardens seem to take pleasure in terrorising him, threatening him with fines if they caught him parked in a residents spot again. This apparently, happened every week and that they should be more understanding of people like him trying to make a living in such hard economic times, economic hardships 'caused by the previous government', he reliably informed Carol.

"Don't make eye contact with him, I'm not getting into a conversation with him about the traffic wardens again," said Carol.

"I think it's his way of chatting you up. You should share your hatred of speed humps with him, he'll go weak at the knees."

"I'm sure he would, come on, before he notices us."

The truth was, as Carol was well aware, the local traffic wardens threatened him for the sole reason of winding him up as they always got a reaction, and it made them laugh. Which was always better than getting shouted at by people who had just got a parking fine, people who *knew* exactly the risk they were taking, parking on a double yellow.

Carol really sympathised with most of the wardens, trying to do their job. The amount of cars in town had become ridiculous. Not the amount in itself, but the amount of chancers. Parking where they knew they were going to cause problems for others.

Carol and Janice left Mansel street, passing the bollards. And started the way down Oakwood Street towards the station. Carol set the pace, because if that was left to Janice she would feel like she was walking backwards. The sky was clear and the weather forecast was set for being dry all day.

"That's a fancy BMW, who's is that then?" asked Janice with her thick Welsh Port Talbot accent, thinking it a bit strange. To give Janice credit she had a gift for noticing things that were out of the ordinary.

"Don't know. It's a fairly new one, let's keep

going," Carol evidently didn't see it as extraordinary.

"It can't be from around here, it has a Wolverhampton Wanderers badge on it," said Janice.

"Maybe it's someone visiting friends," replied Carol.

It already felt warm, Carol didn't want to get a sweat on before they started. They approached the corner of the former police station, now a block of flats and the former bank, now a Pizza Hut. The diggers had long gone now, and a new pedestrianised area had been paved. Almost there.

8.31am

A bus pulled into Swansea bus station.

"Can we go get a coffee please? One that has a loo and we can get something to drink before we start looking."

"You are forever looking for a loo. Do you not think it's a two edged sword going to the loo and then refilling with a diuretic?"

"Please? The sugar and caffeine will help us find it sooner."

"Fine, as long as we aren't going to stop every five minutes to empty your bladder."

"I hope all this running around was worth the early start."

"You know it is and we have obligations, I feel bad enough as it is."

8.37am

The first train of the day had left hours earlier, but for Carol and Janice they had agreed the first train of the day - for them - was the 08.45am to Cardiff Central.

"I wished we had left earlier," said Carol. She shouldn't have to rush the last few minutes, living so close to the station she should be getting there well in time.

8.39am

They entered Port Talbot Parkway. Access to the platforms were, despite the upgrade, still via the stairs up and over. The station had needed updating for years, now the designers had gone for it. What was a modest looking station had now been made to look like the starship Enterprise had had a crash and left a vital booster engine behind. Either that or one of those accessories for a vacuum cleaner, no-one knows what to do with, left somewhere safe, only to chuck them out at a later date long after the vacuum has departed. Made to look like the station of the future, only if the present was the sixties and the future had yet to arrive, but it isn't, it's the 2000's and it actually looks like the future of the past.

8.40am

Janice was out of breath as always, as she reached the top of the steps, before a short walk and then trudged down again as they arrived at platforms 1 and 2. She could take the lift, an easier option, but she viewed taking the steps as her daily workout.

8.42am

Carol was the first to walk down the platform, passing passengers ready to catch the

8.45am. She strained her neck looking ahead to see if they were free. (They were always free) She leaned forward as she walked. Janice just shook her head.

"That's how Dad met his demise," said Janice, raising her voice at Carol some yards ahead. "Worrying about things that don't need worrying about." *'They will be available,'* Janice said to herself, *'they are always available, when, if ever, does Port Talbot Parkway have enough people on it to occupy all the seats....what time is it? 8.43am....two minutes for the train to arrive. It'll be fine. We are here in plenty of time, plenty of time to get ourselves settled for the day. I'm sure she's got OCD.'*

Carol sighed a sigh of relief as she saw the vacant bench facing the town. She sat down and popped her bag between her legs and waited. She looked down the track and she could already see the 8.45am train in the near distance. Janice flumped down at her side.

Pam, who was one of the station staff and a close friend of the women, was on the tannoy already making the announcement of the train's imminent arrival, the stops ahead and what delays could be expected.

The passengers stood up ready to board their train. Some shuffled forward to the edge of the platform. A businessman stood ready to jump on, wearing a grey suit and a white shirt. He had a small but smart black rucksack. His shoes were smart but looked like they were bought for comfort, smart enough for the office, but also practical enough that if a sudden need of speed was required, they would do the job with ease. He was one of the regulars on the platform.

"There he is," said Janice, removing her bobble hat, realising her mistake, as it was warmer than she had expected. "He always looks stressed doesn't he?"

"Oh I know, the train won't depart any sooner."

"He should get an earlier train, at least if he's early he can stop and get himself one of those expensive coffees in whichever city he's going to or a bacon bap. Although if he stopped for a bacon bap everyday he wouldn't look so slim. Do you think he works out?"

"Definitely!" said Carol. "Although if he's a

smoker that might cancel out the bacon bap calories, smokers are almost always slimmer than non smokers."

"Yeah but they die sooner!"

"True. Although our Aunty Doreen smoked like a chimney well into her eighties and she was fit as fiddle, barring the constant smokers cough," said Carol. "Did you know you can get a Greggs app now?"

"Can you?" asked Janice.

"Yeah, it's great if you are a regular visitor. However, every time I go to get my phone scanned I can't seem to get the right angle, either that or the scanner's broken," admitted Carol. "Maybe our friend, even when he is early, is just always anxious to get places."

"Maybe. Maybe he is just a stress head. We should ask him one day what he does, and what he's got in his bag. And maybe his phone number."

"Yeah, whatever!" smirked Carol, "Like you stand a chance. He's just finished hanging out with the 'Milkybar Kid', you might be able to ask for his dad's number but not his."

"Oh thanks. Although you just referenced

the 'Milkybar Kid'. The Milkybar Kid is a historical character. Kids like him studied the Milkybar Kid in school. Really showing your age. Do you want to reference the *Power Rangers* next? Or *Zig'n'Zag* Granny?"

"It's not me that wants his number."

The young man got on the train with all the other passengers and the platform was empty once again.

They both fell silent as they watched the train go off in the distance, they watched as it got smaller and smaller almost until it's out of sight. There's something fascinating watching a train disappearing down a dead straight track, almost entrancing.

A little more silence ensued.

Then suddenly, "Anyway," said Janice. "Have you heard Camila Cabello's new track?"

Carol just looked at her in disbelief and they both erupted in laughter.

"Don't even try and pretend you're with it," laughing as she was speaking, "you've been without '*it*' for some time! You've been listening to Capitol Radio again haven't you? Camila Cabello! Oh my life!"

"What?" said Janice trying her best to do her impression of being sincere, "can't I listen to modern stuff?"

"Oh it's not the listening to modern music that is the issue, it's the trying to drop it casually into conversation, like it's something you know about. You're a riot sometimes." said Carol, shaking her head smiling.

9.03am

The coffee shop wasn't too busy, as the elderly couple finished their drinks.

"Two more minutes and we can start looking."

"Okay, let me use the loo while you finish up. How are we doing with the old coffee loyalty card? When are we due a free one?"

"A couple more yet. Come on, the quicker you go to the loo the quicker we can get started. And if you are a good boy I'll buy you an ice-cream in Verdes once we're done."

"Deal."

"Let's hurry, the bus to the Mumbles leaves soon."

9.32am

It was quiet on the platform, any noise mainly came from the road traffic opposite. It would be a while before the next train. Carol and Janice had no intention of catching any train, they were going to be here for the day.

"Why do you think they hang round here?" asked Janice.

"Who?"

"The pigeons." Like it was obvious Carol would get what she was on about.

A pigeon was strutting on Janice's side of the bench. Carol only spotted it as it strutted around to the front of the bench. It picked up a fag butt and flicked it in the air. *Nope. Not edible. Keep trying, strut, strut, strut, peck, peck, peck.*

"There's nothing here and yet they always turn up looking for stuff," said Janice. "I can understand them making a nest here, 'cause it's dry and out of the rain. I get that, but why not fly off into town, there's always some fat kid stuffing a crumby pastie in his mouth over there, or an old lady flinging chips on the floor for the birds. So why hang round here?"

"Well it's not lunchtime yet. Maybe they have a set routine. Mornings, hang round station, afternoons, get lunch, evenings, trip to the beach." suggested Carol

"I hadn't thought of that. Well let's keep an eye on him or her. How do you tell the difference if it's a he or she?"

"I think the males are usually bigger and puffier chests. The complete opposite of female humans."

"Oh right. Well ok, let's keep an eye on ...him?...and see if he flies off for lunch. It could be some sort of research, if we note it down, we can send our findings off to the RSPCA."

"We? Leave me out of it, don't involve me in your mad research. And it's the RSPB not RSPCA."

"Is there a difference?"

"Yes they are two different organisations, ones for cats and dogs and other animals and the other is for the protection of birds."

"Oh I thought that was the WWE? Or the WWF? Whichever, I thought it was one of them.

Anyway, I'm going to note that down for re-search, is puffier, two f's or one?" Janice pulled out her phone and started making a note.

"Well that'll be an ice-breaker for the Milky-bar Kid's mate, Mr Stresshead. Make sure you spell pigeon correctly otherwise he'll think you're an idiot or something."

"Shut up!"

The pigeon started to suspect he was being talked about, and realised these two women weren't going to share food anytime soon. He strutted up towards a fellow pigeon further up the platform to see if he could find something of any interest up there.

Pigeons weren't the only features of Port Talbot Parkway. It also had toilets, which both sisters were glad about. It made spending time here far more convenient and saved a long walk home. Carol and Janice weren't trainspotters by any means, in fact the trains in themselves weren't of any interest to them. But to them, their *high life* was the luxury of time and being able to spend it people watching and generally observing the world as it passed them by. The station staff had got used to seeing them both here twice a week come rain or shine. In fact at times they've been able to report some of their observations, which have been of real use to the staff.

Once, they heard a plaintive cry from one of the women's toilet cubicles. A lady had gone in and did her business, but the lock got itself stuck and the woman was unable to get out. Ever ready to help, Janice had alerted the staff to the issue and they were able to get the woman out. However the affected lady was totally mortified, not just for getting stuck in the cubicle, but she had evidently been busy and everyone had to try and get her out amongst the smell and haze of her efforts. One of the staff started to gag and to leave the area to gulp down some fresh air.

At other times it had been a case of reporting suspicious items left by passengers, who had usually just forgotten the item. Fortunately there was a lost property for people to collect their items on their return.

Lost property had the usual items sat on a shelf, umbrellas, hats, the odd glove, some false teeth - who forgets their false teeth? Surely that's something you're going to notice at some point. What do you do when you get to your destination and go out for a meal? Or eat anything for that matter? And the fact that they've gone unclaimed was even stranger. Somebody must have had to go back to their dentist for a refit. Somebody even left a black & white tv on the platform, which raises more questions about the person who left it.

Some more passengers had started to arrive ready for the next arrival. Not many, the rush hour was well and truly gone.

"Did Dad ever talk to you about what he was going to do in retirement?" asked Carol. A young mother was adjusting her baby's buggy, something had caught in the handle, at the same time she was making baby talk. Both sisters were watching her.

"No he didn't. I asked him once, but I didn't really get a straight answer. *No point dwelling on that now,* he said *'I haven't thought further than teatime yet'.* I knew that wasn't true, but he evidently wasn't going to entertain me with a proper answer. Did he say anything to you?"

"Well not as such, but a week before he

passed, a National Trust letter came through the door addressed to him. I knew he really wasn't one for subscriptions. When I asked him about what it was. He said he had paid for a years membership to the National Trust, it included a newsletter and free parking to most sites around the country. So I assume he was planning some days out."

The young mother had got herself sorted and now full attention was being given to her baby.

"Oh I didn't know that. I wonder where he would have gone? He talked of Croft Castle once in Herefordshire, that's National Trust. He mentioned it had a cafe and toilets, *'so would be a good place to go'* he said. Emphasis on there being toilets."

"Oh yeah that would make sense," Janice acknowledged. "Do you remember we went to Swansea once and he got caught short. I've never seen him look so stressed trying to find a loo. He found one place, only to find it was shut and the next was closed for cleaning. We had to persuade him to go to McDonald's, but he didn't want to go because he didn't want to buy anything from there. He eventually had to admit defeat as his bladder had raised the stakes in a weird game of chicken."

"Oh yes, while he went to the toilet, we promptly joined the food queue. Mam saw what we were up to,thought this was hilarious and joined us in ordering a 'Meal Deal' each. Did you see Dad's face when he realised we had committed to paying for our food?"

"Yes, his face was a picture." responded Janice, "especially when we sat down to eat and put a happy meal in front of him. To be fair he did find the funny side, as he pulled out the toy and couldn't help but laugh seeing he'd been had."

"That was such a great day out, have you still got the Happy Meal toy?"

"Yes, it's still there on the shelf."

The next train approached the platform.

"Oh, oh," said Carol. The young mother had now picked up her baby, just as the train was coming up the tracks, and baby took the opportunity to empty the contents of its stomach all over her mother's top. How could so much come out of something so small?

With her hands full the mother looked up the track and then back at her top trying to desperately assess the situation. Janice quickly leaped into action, as if she had anticipated the event, pulled out a pack of tissues, and ran to help the mother.

"Hold on love, here we are," Janice said. "Here's some tissues." She knew if they get the majority off the mothers top and the buggy folded, mother and baby could make it on the train and mother would have time to sort herself out properly once seated.

Pam, who had left her tannoy duties and had not long been on the platform, was already making her way to help with the buggy anyway, but vomit had added jeopardy to the situation. Once she realised what had happened she quickly got on the radio to buy a minute or two to resolve the situation.

"Bill, get onto the driver and get him to wait a minute, we have a minor situation," she said into a radio.

"Oh thank you," said the mother, "you guys are life savers."

"Hey, no problem," said Pam, "if baby was

going to throw up any time, it was going to be now, wasn't it?"

"Absolutely, she has a knack. I'll just get myself a new top at my stop." The mother said, wiping the remainder off her and the baby.

"Here, put the tissues in here," said Janice, offering an open carrier bag, "I'll get rid of that for you."

"You're very kind, thank you both again," said the mother.

Pam assisted her and baby onto the train, drama done and dusted. Janice watched as the door was shut behind here and the train slowly pulled away.

"Well done Pam," commended Janice.

"Teamwork makes the dream work J," said Pam. "Give me the bag, I'll pop it in the bin on my way back to the office.

"You're a lovely person Pam, no matter what others say, thanks."

"I know, just don't spread it around," Pam said, smiling as she headed back down the platform.

Janice then turned and made her way back to her position.

"Well that was almost a disaster, poor girl. She said it happens all the time at exactly the wrong moments," said Janice glad to have been able to help. "Right, I think I deserves a coffee after that." She pulled out a flask with a tartan pattern on. It's the one her mother used to use on family days out. However, instead of using the plastic cup the flask came with, she preferred to use a normal ceramic mug from the house.

Carol looked up to the clock, 9.35am, "That sounds like a plan, I'll join you."

The morning was warming up, the sun had been out all morning and the trend was showing promise of unbroken sunshine to follow. Janice's pigeon was showing no intention of leaving any time soon, but it was still the morning, so plenty of time to continue the morning routine.

However it hadn't gone unnoticed that coffee had been brought out, which means biscuits might appear. *Time to wander back, I thinks. Never know, might get lucky, and I wouldn't want to miss out on any biscuit action. Just act cool.*

They sat quietly drinking their coffees,

Janice had her's white with no sugar, whilst Carol had hers black. Both agreed it had to be nice coffee as cheap coffee could be too bitter and burnt too easily to have it black. Neither considered themselves coffee snobs, it didn't have to be some special blend hand picked by natives from a far flung area of the world, just a nice flavour.

Janice's pigeon had started making his way back towards the pair on the bench, he was now being followed by his lady friend who wasn't going to let him have all the fun. *'Why is he trying to act cool?' she said to herself, 'They are definitely going to know exactly what he is up to. Plonker!'*

"Here comes your friend again. I bet he wants breakfast," said Carol, nodding her head towards the two pigeons.

"Yeah, and he's attracted attention from his lady friend, she's in hot pursuit."

"Well he's going to be a bit disappointed, it's too early for biscuits."

"Make sure you put a note on your phone for your report."

"Good point, I'll note the time and behaviour. That one is a she isn't it?"

As she was making her note, they both noticed the freight train coming down the track. These were always impressive coming through. They seem to go on forever, with one massive diesel engine at the front, a huge train of carriages, followed by an engine at the rear. Both sisters prepared themselves for the noise. The pigeons didn't seem to care too much, although they seemed to strut to a safer distance from the platform's edge. Well behind the yellow line at least.

The noise died down as the leviathan made its way down the track. The next train wasn't expected for a while, so the two women just sipped their coffee.

Lost in their thoughts. The hills opposite made a nice view behind the buildings of the town. When the sun shone brightly like today, the hills shone too. They were substantial, not impressive in size, but big enough to act as a beautiful backdrop to what was essentially a cramped industrial town. Too small to be classified as mountains, but big enough to be considered hills.

All the hills in the surrounding area were steep with flattish tops, where the walking was easy and the views rewarding. On days like to-day, looking south you were greeted with a flat landscape that met the sea. From such a height the buildings look tiny and cars are like ants that follow a well trodden route.

They went with their dad one winter time around the top of Dinas Mountain (as the locals call it, very liberal with the word mountain). They started out at the farm where it was leafy and autumnal, as they walked around the south side layers of clothing were removed as the sun blazed, which didn't last long. Following the track east, they felt the temperature cool more like spring, layers were put back on. After which, for the rest of the journey on the north side and then westwards was spent trudging through two inches of snow. And then back to the autumnal side to return to the car.

Not today though, the sun had risen very quickly and was becoming much warmer than anticipated. Carol and Janice were no longer wearing their jackets. The hills seemed to reflect the sunshine back at them. It was turning out to be a very pleasant day.

"I bet you Mr Stresshead has already arrived at his destination," suggested Janice.

"Where do you think he was going?"

"Well I don't know obviously, but he seemed to leave too late to make it worthwhile going to London. London would be too far and Bridgend would seem too close to be worth going to by train, so I would assume Cardiff Central or Newport. That and if he was going to London he would need an overnight bag, but he only had a small rucksack. So I should think he's already arrived and making his way to the office."

"Maybe," agreed Carol.

"Hey, maybe he works for the BBC, they've got those new buildings right opposite Cardiff Central Station. Perhaps he's a journalist of some kind, trying to get the daily scoop for the News. You never know, maybe that's why he looked like a stresshead." Janice was well away now, her imagination running wild. "Maybe he had some story he needed to report, some dodgy dealings going down. Maybe some informant has grassed up a local drug barren and the police are about to make a coordinated raid on multiple properties. In an operation they've called 'Operation Daffodil'. He's at his BBC desk right now typing frantically in time for the afternoon news. The editor is breathing down his neck to get it written up ASAP. If we put on the one o'clock news we'll see it being read out. Perhaps I should put a reminder on my phone and we can watch it on Iplayer."

Carol interrupted, "Ok I agree he could have gone to Cardiff, but as soon as he steps out of the station, the one thing he isn't doing is rushing towards a BBC hot desk with a drug bust report for the one o'clock news. And nobody is going to care about a drugs raid in Port Talbot, let alone call it 'Operation Daffodil'. Anyway, how many drug barrens do you think are wandering Port Talbot? There's hardly going to be some 'El Chapo' style drugs cartel round here. I saw Bernie the other day with a dodgy moustache, I know he's a dealer, but hardly a big name. It's not exactly the badlands round here is it?"

"Well it's not out of the question, you

know," protested Janice, "What about 'Mr Nice'? Howard Marks, isn't he from South Wales?"

"Yes, Bridgend."

"Well there you go then, he was an international drugs barren. He dealt in millions of pounds worth of drugs. And that was millions in the seventies, with inflation that would be much more now. So you never know, there could be an 'Operation Daffodil' going down right under our noses and we wouldn't hear about it until it was reported on the news the following day. And just to think we were yards away from the journalist who had the scoop."

"OK, well put that reminder on your phone and we'll put the news on and see if it comes up."

"You're on," replied Janice, thumbing her phone, looking for the clock app.

"What time is it now?" asked Carol

"Just gone ten, ages yet before the next one,"

"Don't forget I want to listen to pop master at 10.30!"

"I'll put a reminder for that as well."

"Good idea," said Carol.

10.08am

More passengers had arrived on the platform in time for the 10.11am train.

A group of retired pensioners emerged from the stairs. Each was dressed like they were in the Scouts. Everyone had a hikers waterproof jacket and a backpack each. One backpack had a collection of laminated walking routes neatly tucked in a pocket. All had walkers poles, not walking sticks, like old peoples walking sticks. Oh no! These were your proper hikers poles with shock absorbers, lightweight, adjustable, aircraft grade aluminium, all terrain, walkers poles, essential for the serious walker. Armed with their senior railcards, they were ready for their day out.

"I bet you the one with the maps stuffed in his backpack is the leader, he looks eager," observed Carol.

"Huh, yeah. He's the one who has learnt how to use the interweb and sent an itinerary via email. The times, prices, who's coming. And I bet the portly one, is one who's organised the group discount meal and drinks at the watering hole at the end of their walk. He just looks the type. His cheeks are red before they've started."

"There's ten of them. Where do you suppose they're going? It can't be a long walk or that far away."

"Taffs trail?" suggested Janice. "That's a nice walk and you can get there from Central station. Or maybe they'll get off at Bridgend and use their bus passes to do a coastal walk, Ogmore by sea or somewhere round there."

"Good thinking, and you can get there relatively quickly so it's not too late to do a walk and get back before dark."

"Do you reckon they all went to the Mountain Outdoors Equipment shop together or do you think they are into online shopping?" asked Janice.

Carol gave this a little thought and after some deliberation said, "I reckon they all went to the Mountain Outdoors Equipment shop. *'You can't trust the quality off the internet you know, and what if you want to return something?'*" She did her best posh elderly woman's voice as she said it.

Janice joined in, "Can you imagine the

manager's face as they walked in? He would have been dreaming what he was going to spend his commission on before they would have spent a penny of their pensions. *'Oh yes madam, you can't trust the internet. You get cold you say. Well we don't refer to grades of material as denier anymore, but I'm sure this really expensive genuine hikers jacket with plentiful pockets for your wallet, phone and pills will be the right one for you. What do you know? It fits you perfectly, it's made you look so much younger. Would you like these hikers poles to go with that? Yes we sell whistles, would you like a compass too? They are on offer this month. Now, do you have proper footwear madam? Walk this way and bring your friend, she'll love these.'* KACHING!, I bet he got manager of the month after they had gone, followed by a promotion to the area sales team.

"It's really nice though. It must be uplifting to spend time with like minded people even if some are more officious than others. I bet there's one or two widows and widowers amongst them. They've decided to fight the loneliness and replace it with a walking group. Walking, talking and having a lovely meal with others is better than feeling sorry for ones-self in an empty house. Especially on a day like to-day," mused Carol.

"I guess. I wonder if they are a part of some other groups or clubs."

"Would you want to join a club of some sort?" asked Carol.

"I don't know, I've never given it much thought. I guess I've never felt the urge. I don't have that kind of void to fill. I like people, don't get me wrong, but I'm not looking to spend my time with others in a group situation. What about you?"

"I did look one time, but it's all charity groups and Slimming World around here. Otherwise it's all online stuff which I'm definitely not into. I don't want to spend social time staring at a screen. Although I did think of maybe doing some sort of course at Afan College."

"What, like brick-laying or woodwork?"

"Yeah, just like those! Can you see me trying to lay a brick?" said Carol, "no, like a language or textiles, not to get a qualification, but just for fun. You know, maybe an evening class or something."

"Well that sounds good, I bet you would enjoy a class like those."

10.09am

Map leader guy was now organising the troops, he was pointing out it was 10.09am and the train would be arriving soon. "Two minutes everyone," he announced. They dutifully started to line themselves behind the yellow line and they all were glancing down the track waiting for the train to come into sight. He had them well drilled. One of the group could be heard asking if there was a toilet on board, she did go before she left the house but she thought the latte she had enroute was now taking effect. No-one really knew, but if not, maybe there would be at the other station. She wasn't sure if she could last that long, but agreed it was too late to make a mad dash to the toilets here. Especially by the time she loosened all the bits she needed to, just to go and then get herself together again before boarding.

The train slowly pulled in and came to a halt. Map Guy opened the door and ushered everyone in and shouted instructions as regards seating, before getting on himself. A couple of other passengers got on and the 10.11am pulled away, taking the cast of Cacoon with it.

"Well that was a little eventful," said Janice as the station went quiet again. Phil, one of the other platform staff, could be seen sweeping the platform at the far end. The toilets would need a refresh soon.

10.10am

"Are you okay? We've only been in Mumbles ten minutes."

"Can we sit down for five? It's warm already, I wasn't expecting it to be this warm so early in the day, I could do with something to eat too."

"Yes, sure, you wait here and I'll get us some bacon baps."

"You are a mind reader, thanks love, brown sauce please."

"It's a good job I brought your medication, you aren't as strong as you used to be. You'll feel a bit better once you've had your pills and something to eat."

"I'm still good looking though? Right?"

"Absolutely, from the neck up, I can't stop looking at you. But your ability to carry that box, if we find it, from place to place is looking a bit ropey, we need to get you back to the gym."

"Probably best to avoid the gym, I wouldn't want to embarrass the younger guys when they see my physique."

"That's very thoughtful of you. Keep having a think where we might have left the box while I get the baps."

"I reckon we only have a couple of places I could have left it, then maybe we can head back to check the Marina."

10.12am

Carol stood up. She'd been sat down since they arrived. "I'm just going to wander down to the end of the platform, I'm getting a bit stiff sat down."

"Ok old girl. Do you want your zimmer or do you think you'll be ok?"

"Funny! Don't let me miss 'Pop Master'."

"Righto! No problem. I'll sit here awaiting your return." Janice said reassuringly.

Carol made her way down the platform, out of the shade of the shelter and into the sunshine. *'What a difference'*, she thought, *'That's really nice.'* As the warmth of the sun gently hit her skin. It was just the right temperature, a heat that could be enjoyed all day long. But it wasn't even lunchtime yet and it would only get warmer. And the temperature would rise to one that could still be enjoyed, but would need a bit of sunscreen and maybe only for about thirty minutes at a time. She stretched her arms out and arched her back as she walked, and let out a sigh that was more revealing of her age than she would like to admit to.

No trains were due for a while. She enjoyed the momentary solitude as she looked up the track and then let her eyes scan the surroundings bathed in sunshine. Moments like these were to be savoured, as these kinds of days weren't a regular event, so needed to be taken advantage of in the moment. On days like today everyone seemed more relaxed, a bit more laid back. Even the traffic seemed less hectic, less in a hurry, with the odd tune beating out the open windows. Even the vehicles with air-con took the opportunity to drive with windows down. You can see why those who live in sunnier climes live at a slower pace.

Sunshine like today made her more nostalgic. Taking her back to her childhood, and everyone knows rain didn't exist back in their childhood and sunny days lasted forever. At age nine or ten she remembered being told to get out and play and not to spend all day indoors. She'd go up towards Felindre and spend her time in the river opposite the school. Hours would be spent overturning rocks looking for bullfish, she had no idea at the time if that was what they were actually called, but they were black with bulbous heads and hid under the rocks, (years later she discovered they were actually called Bullheads and the black ones were males). Once all the Bullheads had been scared off and had to find new locations to hide, there was only one other option, in order to entertain herself.

With so many stones and pebbles just laying there waiting to be thrown, it would have been rude not to, what child would refuse this golden opportunity. And like every other child who has the opportunity to throw stones, even this activity could be split into sub-activities of high value entertainment.

The first was to find a stone that would create the biggest splash, and this would only continue until both arms had become exhausted. So a more lighter option would now need to be taken up.

So the next game would be to choose a stone that could be thrown as high as it would go and then provide the smallest splash possible, again this would be done until the throwing arm had once again become exhausted. A small rest sat on a boulder would be needed for some restbite before the main event, a more technical affair, requiring dexterity, the ability to count, as well as understanding the physical properties of the stones needed for the next activity. Stone skimming!

Now, this is a whole world of its own. Choosing the correct stone for the job at hand was to be taken seriously. Using an almost forensic method of searching the bankside, a flattish smooth stone would be selected. If the stone was too irregular or fat then you would only be setting yourself up for disappointment, with only yourself to blame. The result would be some sort of bellyflop of the stone world, and it would immediately crash into the riverbed. The correct stone would also need to fit into the hand. Grip was key, with your index finger needed to wrap around the circumference of the stone for best traction. So once the correct weight, size and shape criteria had been met. Technique was the next key element. A smooth horizontal swing of the entire arm, with power generated from the shoulder. A bend of the knees is essential, with your body adjacent to the direction of the throw. But all of this would be of no use if an intense flick of the wrist wasn't given. At the last moment the wrist would flick and the index finger would transfer all the power, speed and traction into the stone. The whole motion once mastered was an elegant one, body, arm, finger and stone as one. As the stone left the hand it hit the water, spinning as it did so bouncing again and again and again.

The more bounces that resulted from each

throw, the greater the feeling of achievement was felt.

Carol's consciousness was dragged back to the present day, like a loved one being called back from a coma. Janice's voice had managed to penetrate Carol's nostalgic train of thought.

"Two minute warning, 'Pop Master' will be starting soon. Ken has already given the big build up."

Whilst Carol had been lost in the past while having a little stretch, Janice had managed to open up the radio app. Ken Bruce was the only daytime programme either of the two women could tolerate. Some DJ's were like ground-hog day after tedious day, same format, same possy, same jokes, still talking over the music, factoids that no one was verifying. Spreading mis-information to builders and taxi drivers everywhere. It was fun at first but decades later he's still doing the same gig. With co presenters unable to find other employment it seems.

"Hello, We have John Walters from Cirences-ter on the line ready to do 'Pop Master', hello John." Carol is back and sat down ready for the quiz to begin.

"Oh hello Ken, how are you?"

"Yes I'm doing well, what do you do there in Cirencester?"

"Ken is so good at making contestants comfortable isn't he? I think it's his Scottish accent." said Janice.

"Well I'm not originally from Cirencester Ken, I'm a data analyst for a local company that provides statistical information for companies interested in improving performance, I'm originally from Solihull Ken."

"Do you have any family?"

"Oh yes Ken, my wife is working from home, so she's upstairs listening with our dog."

"Oh what kind of dog do you have?"

"Oh yes, what kind of dog?" repeated Janice.

"It's a Maliwawa Ken, it's a cross between a Malamute and a Chiwawa."

"A what?!" exclaimed Carol

"Goodness me, how'd that happen?"

"Oh don't ask Ken, the story is, the owners of the Chiwawa were a bit careless when their dog got away from them in a park. Soon after they discovered she was pregnant, once the puppies were born they did a doggy DNA test and the other half came back as Malamute. The physics don't bear thinking about Ken."

"Indeed, that would have certainly brought a tear to the eye for the Chiwawa in that relationship. Anyway, are you ready for your questions?"

"As ready as I'll ever be Ken."

"For your bonus questions you can choose between 'types of fruit in songs' or Gerry Rafferty."

"I don't know much about Gerry Rafferty, so I'll have to choose 'types of fruit in songs' Ken."

"Okay, let's..play.... 'Pop Master'! Good Luck!"

"I'll bet you Prince will be one the answers." said Janice.

"So for 3 points The Darts had a hit in 1978 with 'Come back my love', what position did it peak in the charts?"

"No.2," Carol said as quickly as she could.

"No.2 Ken."

"In which year did Duran Duran have their first major hit 'Girls on Film'?"

"1985," blurted Janice.

"1982 Ken."

"Ohh, one year out, hard luck 1981 was the

answer. Now here comes your first bonus question on 'types of fruit in songs'.

"Fantastic, he'll get a 'one year out t-shirt for that.' said Janice

"For six points, who had a hit with Raspberry Beret?"

"I knew it." Janice said, clapping her hands.

"That'll be Prince Ken."

Janice bent down and pulled her bag forward, Janics's pigeon and girlfriend both recognised the noise and they strutted quickly from behind Carol and Janice. They were both in sync, with Janice's pigeon slightly ahead.

She pulled out a pack of biscuits. And started to open them.

"Sshhh," said Carol, "it's his second bonus question."

Janice waited for the question to be asked and the answer to be given "Banana Pancakes Ken," she quickly pulled the packet open. And waited for the next opportune moment to pull a biscuit out. The two pigeons had made their way directly in front of Janice without any sort of embarrassment, there was no pretence as to why they were there. Discretion wasn't a life skill given to pigeons, so not only was it obvious to the biscuit handler, but their earnestness had attracted the attention of a couple of other pigeons, who up until now had been combing the platform elsewhere. They glided in, flapped to a landing and continued with a strut which drew the attention of one other pigeon. All five were now turning this way and that ready for any biscuit action.

"Well after ten questions your final score is 27, not bad, a decent effort. How do you feel about that?"

"It's a lot harder on the radio Ken but yes I'm chuffed with that Ken, I was glad to get a question right in the end."

"Well stay on the line, we have Paul Hanson coming on next to see if he can beat John's score of 27. After we have heard Camila Cabello's latest release."

"In your face, I am with it!" exclaimed Janice, "Come on Camila."

"Forget that, give us a biscuit."

Janice started to pull out a biscuit, the pigeons by now were working themselves into a frenzy. She handed Carol the packet of biscuits and holding the packet carefully in her hand so as not to let any biscuits fall out, tipped any loose crumbs from the packet letting them fall to the ground. Wow, the moment they had all been waiting for, and they wasted no time. Each bird's sole attention was given to spotting every orange crumb on the floor.

Carol poured herself another cup of coffee before the second round.

"Good idea," said Janice, "How do you think Paul Hanson is going to do?"

"I reckon mid to late teens, 15? 18? Depends what his bonus questions are. John's bonus questions were quite easy I thought." She said, sipping her coffee. She picked up the packet of biscuits again and pulled out three biscuits.

10.39am

Some more passengers had arrived on the platform ready for the 10.42am train.

The two women hadn't taken too much notice of them, as they had been concentrating on the 'PopMaster' questions.

A young couple with suitcases had made

their way up the platform. They looked like they were heading on their holidays. They checked the platform clock. 10.39am. Both had their phones in hand and giving cursory glances up the track. A voice from above informed all passengers that the 10.42am train was running a couple of minutes late.

"We now have Paul Hanson from Harrow on the line, how are you Paul?"

"A little nervous Ken, but fine, how are you?"

"Why do they always ask Ken how he is, they know how he is, he said earlier?" said Carol.

"I'm absolutely fine, What keeps you busy in Harrow Paul?"

"I'm a sky-diving instructor Ken."

"In Harrow? Is there much call for that in North London?"

"That's exactly what I would say my job was, If I was on 'PopMaster', anything has to be better than data analyst." said Janice.

"Not much Ken, no. But I travel to an airfield not too far away and teach people who want to learn how to skydive and I also teach others who want to become instructors themselves. So if you ever fancy a try Ken give me a call."

"That's very kind of you Paul, but I wouldn't want to show you up. Do you have any family and friends listening in this morning?"

Despite the announcement the 10.42am was coming down the line just about on time. The train drowned out the rest of the conversation between Ken and Paul. Carol and Janice watched the passengers board the train, sipping their coffee and making their way through the HobNobs as they did so. The pigeons were still milling around in the hope of a further windfall of crumbs.

The doors of the train were closed as the train's engines intensified as it slowly pulled off from the station continuing it's journey eastwards. As it did and far too late for it to stop, a man came rushing down the steps only to come to a complete stop, as he realised his efforts to be on time were wasted. The irony being he would have made it if the train had actually come late as announced.

"I have got to go to the loo." said Janice as she finished her coffee. "I'll be back in a mo, let me know how Paul does, and make a note if he gives his mobile number out live on air. I have an urge to go sky-diving."

"Don't worry I'm poised and ready."

"Question 3, for your bonus questions you chose 'Artists from the noughties.'"

"He's got no chance. Paul you've had it." she said, addressing the phone.

"Who in the noughties had a track entitled, 'Jenny Don't be Hasty'?"

"He's no chance, the answer is Paulo Nutini, but he won't get it."

"Oh I'm sorry Ken, the Arctic Monkeys Ken?"

"What did I say?!"

"No, it was Paulo Natini, question 4 for a further 3 points."

"Private Dancer was written by Mark Knoffler for which female artist?"

"Bonnie Tyler Ken."

"Hopeless, Tina Turner! Everyone knows it's Tina Turner. You've lost this mate, you better have your list ready to say hello to your family, friends and everyone else who knows you Paul."

Carol poured herself a top up, and helped herself to another biscuit. Fortunately neither Janice or Carol were calorie counters. Which was probably a good thing given the glut of calories in each biscuit.

Carol lost interest in Paul, she answered most of the questions that were left.

"Well at the end of those questions Paul you only managed 9 points, hard luck, it wasn't quite your day today."

"No Ken, I did better on John's questions, but I think nerves got the better of me Ken. All the best to John for 3 in 10."

"That's generous of you, you'll get a 'one year out' t-shirt, would you like to say hello to anyone whilst you are on?"

"Thank you Ken."

Carol mentally switched off as Paul rattled off his hellos and threw a few more crumbs down for the pigeons.

Janice was not going to make it back in time for 3 in 10.

"Well done, congratulations on winning today's 'PopMaster', you are through to 3 in 10."

"Nope, I was wrong," said Carol in her head. Janice was hurrying back.

"Did I miss 3 in 10? Who won in the end?"

Carol put her finger to her lips and flapped the hand for Janice to be quiet.

"Give me three hits for Sophie Ellis-Bexter."

"Murder on the Dance Floor," said Janice, feeling the pressure. "Oh I Know It, 'Take me home...Oh..oh."

"Umm Umm I can't think Ken."

"Hard luck there you couldn't quite get the last one...," Janice closed the app.

"He got the same two as me then, I thought I had it today. What happened to Paul the sky-diver?"

"He was rubbish, he got nine points. I hope he's better at sky-diving."

"Oh that's disappointing, I had high hopes for him." Janice poured herself another coffee and took the last of the HobNobs. "Cor we've murdered that packet of biscuits." She tipped the rest of the crumbs on the floor causing another frenzy. She screwed up the wrapping and popped it in the bin and sat down again. "You should apply for PopMaster, show them how it's done."

"I really couldn't be bothered, and even if I did I don't think I'd have a long enough list of people to say hello to. It would be you, Sally next-door and Pam at a stretch."

"Fair enough," replied Janice.

It wasn't even 11am yet, the next train would be due some time in the next half hour.

The weather had really warmed up. When the two women set out this morning it was a lot fresher. But it was turning out even warmer than Derek 'the Weatherman Walking' had predicted.

"Right then," Janice said emphatically. "All the pigeons have had breakfast, let me make another note on my phone, and then let's see if they head off into town for lunch, and then we'll know."

"We'll know what?"

"Whether they have a routine or not. Either way I'll send my findings to the RSP.....B?"

"You are absolutely mad, do you know that?" Carol had tried to feign disinterest, but she was now totally invested in this mad venture. "Ok, what time do you think they'll go for lunch if at all? I can't believe I'm going along with this."

"I reckon 11.45am, that way they can be there in good time including travel time."

Carol smiled and said, "How do they know what time it is? And have they adjusted for British summer time? 'Cause that could throw their timings out."

"And I'm being daft? There's a clock up there, they can totally tell what time it is. They are modern pigeons after all."

"Oh yeah, silly me."

A seagull seemed to find all this amusing, as it cried aloud from its lamp-post. Although it's not unusual to hear seagulls all day long.

"Like I said before," started Janice, "I can understand pigeons have their reasons for hanging around the station, me being here the obvious one, but what other reasons do seagulls have to hang around here. If I was a seagull, I don't think I would hang around Port Talbot Parkway, as lovely as it is."

"Well you sort of have the same freedoms as that seagull and yet, here you are."

"True, I never thought of it like that."

"Anyway," said Carol, "there are no such things as seagulls."

"Shut up! I can see one from here. There it goes."

"Nope, that is no seagull. There are eleven types of gull in the UK and not one is known as a seagull, they simply don't exist."

"How on earth do you know that and even remember that stuff?"

"If I knew how I remembered where I knew everything from, that would take up twice as much room in my brain, and I don't think I have that sort of capacity. I think it's nearly full, and I think your responsible for filling much of it with junk like these theories about pigeons. And to answer the other half of your question, I read it on the RSPCA's website about gulls."

"You mean the RSPB's?!"

"No," said Carol, "I read on the RSPCA's website."

"What on earth are they writing about birds for? I thought they dealt with cats and dogs and other animals. They ought to be careful they don't step on the RSPB's toes or is that talons. They could start a turf war."

"You should tell them, send them an email. I'm sure they would appreciate the feedback expressing your concerns."

"I'll compile my report for the RSPB first and maybe do that later," replied Janice.

10.55am

"Are you sure this is Promenade Terrace?"

"Yes, very sure, Mr Wallace lives just up here."

"I would have thought he would have con-tacted us if he had come across the box."

"Let's check anyway, we can then rule him out."

"Okay, that's something I suppose. Can we then get some indigestion tablets? I'm not sure white bread agrees with me, you know. I suspect those baps have something to do with my IBS."

"You are such a romantic, you say the nicest things."

11am

The orange digital clock changed from 10.59.00 to 11.00.00.

Some other passengers had turned up and sat down on the benches, giving each other plenty of personal space. They had settled down for the short wait for the next train, thumbing their phones. One young woman opened a book and started reading, pulling out the marker where she had left off.

"Do you remember when we were young, we didn't have smartphones?" started Janice.

"Yes, why?"

"Well I remember, when I got my first mobile phone, I was so excited. I remember I had to buy a ten pound top up card for it. I didn't know who I was going to ring on it, and texting wasn't a thing."

"Right?"

"Well I don't know," Janice mused, "it's sad we all spend hours on smartphones now. The phones have got smarter, but we all look dumber, pawing away at the tiny screens. If I saw someone stroking a telephone when I was younger I would wonder if that person was okay or needed help."

"So you would give yours up would you?" smiled Carol knowing what answer she'd get.

"Absolutely not! This is my porthole to the wider world," Janice replied, clutching it to her chest.

"Well then, what are you moaning about?".

"I know, I know. But look at everyone," she said, nodding in the direction of everyone sat down and lowering her voice a little. "Nobody is talking to one another, it never used to be that way. Everyone seems afraid to make eye contact with the person nearest them. I've had more eye contact with those pigeons".

The young woman with the book pulled out a pack of cigarettes and padded her pockets, searching for a lighter.

"She looks too young to smoke," said Janice.

"Yes, that's because we're getting old. It's one of the main signs of ageing. Policemen, nurses etc. they all look younger as we get older. Although I bet she's been puffing away since she was twelve, the same as some of the girls we were with in school."

"Oh yeah, true. Do you remember the twins in school Hailey and Helen, the only way I could tell one apart from the other is because one smoked and the other didn't. Although now I can't remember which was which."

"I remember them," said Carol. "You know the other way you could tell them apart?"

"How?"

"Well, one was pushing a pram and the other wasn't."

"What? I don't remember that. One had a baby?" said Janice.

"Well she wasn't pushing a pram for no reason. Admittedly not in school hours. Do you remember Stuart? Tall, lanky, looked like a Bash Street Kid?"

"What? He was the father?" said Janice in disbelief. Carol raised her eyebrows and nodded. "But he didn't talk to anyone, he was so shy."

"I know," continued Carol, "you have to watch the quiet ones. I think the baby in the pram works in Wilkos now. Her parents live down Fairway. I passed their house the other day. They are still together. The front door was open, it looks like they have grandchildren too. A couple of staffies were running round the front. He looks less like a Bash Street Kid, still tall and lanky though. She's put on a lot of weight, gravity hasn't been kind to her either."

"Well," said Janice, "happens to us all, I guess. Gravity has a crafty way of sneaking up on you. One minute you are walking around with everything in its proper place and then suddenly the next thing you know it's like someone has shoved a magnet below your bum cheeks."

"True. They should put funding into researching reversing the effects of gravity on certain parts of the human body. Nevermind the space programmes, there are more fundamental, more serious issues here on earth. I'd certainly volunteer myself as a case study," said Carol.

"If you die before that research begins would you like to freeze your body and donate it to science for that purpose?"

"Definitely!" replied Carol.

"Although, I'm not sure there would be enough funding to put all your bits back in the right place even if they could. Or enough power in the grid. They would need more power than that thingamejig collider in Switzerland. And you wouldn't want that plugged in the wrong place neither."

"Well that might be true, but even if they could do a partial reversing of gravity, imagine the overall benefits to humankind. They might even erect a statue of me in honour of my dedication to the cause and how gorgeous I looked. And I would look gorgeous as a statue."

"Well I wouldn't argue with that. I can imagine people walking past and weeping, touched by your beauty and elegance," said Janice smiling.

"They do that now," said Carol.

11.11am

The 11.13am train would be due in a few minutes and some of the passengers were starting to stir and get themselves ready in anticipation of the train's arrival.

"Where would you want this statue to be?" asked Janice.

"Good question. Well, If you put it too close to the main road it might cause an accident as people turned and stared in amazement. So maybe instead of the Civic Centre fountain in the middle of town, prominent enough to be seen and admired, but in a place where there will be less health and safety involvement."

"That is so thoughtful of you. And...And people would be able to have the opportunity to walk around it, viewing its voluptuous beauty from all angles. With a small plaque which would read *'Carol Sanders, a Port Talbot girl who donated her body to medical science for the greater good. You look good thanks to her self-less sacrifice. May she live long in the memory'*," said Janice.

"Very poetic. I love it. Put that down in your notes on your phone. We can prepare a proposal ready for the council, so they can start preparation now. And also a proposal to the scientific community raising awareness of the damaging effects of gravity on the human body and how we urgently need a solution. And my willingness to donate my once gorgeous body to them for research purposes."

"On it!" said Janice emphatically. "I may need help with some of the spelling, but we can iron that out later. Do you want me to prioritise which bits you want them to start on first? Or just leave it up to them?"

"Oh leave it up to them for definite. They are the experts after all."

"True, I'll make a note of your wishes. You are so self-sacrificing." observed Janice.

"Thank you."

In the meantime the young woman had managed to find her lighter, and was already three quarters of the way through her cigarette. She started to puff harder and longer as the train approached the platform. She took one last drag and flicked the butt onto the tracks. The rest of the passengers were readying themselves, shuffling closer to the yellow line and hoping they don't have to walk too far to open the carriage door.

"I hate it when smokers do that," said Janice. "Just flicking their fag ends everywhere." Carol didn't respond, she just watched the passengers board the train.

Pam appeared and looked up and down the platform to see if all was ok before the train departed. As it disappeared into the distance the two women remained in silence for a bit, as they got lost in their own thoughts.

Janice, looking at the platform pigeons, was transported back to a trip to Trafalgar square in London. It was a time when there were pigeons everywhere, and vendors sold bird feed. She remembered her mother buying the bird feed as her dad protested saying *'it's a waste of money, and they will only poo all over you.'* They duly ignored his moaning and opted for a fun photo of herself covered in pigeons. Carol had the camera ready for the shot and she posed like a scare-crow. Her mother poured bird seed into the palms of her hands and across her arms and on her head. And sure enough she was mobbed by the pigeons. She remembered trying to keep still as feathers slapped her in the face. But just as Carol pressed the trigger on the camera, one feathered friend left a wet brown and white deposit down her face and another running down her top.

The final picture, which was developed only after they had returned home, a time before instant smartphone pictures, was of her screaming in blind panic covered in bird poo, in what seemed to be a cloud of pigeons and bird feed confetti. Carol had commented it turned out better than she could ever have hoped for. What wasn't captured in the moments that followed, was her crying in shock and embarrassment as her mother tried to wipe her down with some wet-wipes, as pigeons continued to try for a mouthful of bird seed off her head. Only to pluck strands of hair in their beaks, which added to the misery. With mutterings from their prophetic dad, as he had forewarned such a disaster. Although later he did admit the picture was worth every penny and a memory of a fantastic day out.

Carol meanwhile had a message from the window cleaner, informing her, her windows had been cleaned and payment was due. And payment could be made with the following on-line bank details. She opened up her banking app and made payment straight away. She hated being late making payments. It was like a small weight around her neck. She definitely takes after her dad she admitted. Window cleaners had become so efficient these days. Even the use of technology had entered the world of window cleaning with their fancy poles and on-line banking.

As she pressed the confirm button for pay-ment she remembered an old window cleaner that used to clean windows in her grandpar-ents' street. He wore these thick lens glasses, he wasn't a young man. He carried a heavy wooden frame ladder from another time, even though lighter aluminium ladders had been invented. He also had an old fashioned shammy leather cloth or chamois if you were posh. He wasn't posh, so yeah a shammy cloth, a piece of material that had seen better days. Frayed at the edges and mainly black from cleaning the old cheap rubber around the pvc windows. His bucket of water was no better. At one time it did have detergent in it, if that was the case, then that had long departed. Her grandfather was sure he must have been using pond water, it was so dirty.

She remembered they called him 'Port-hole Bill'. Not because his name was William, Will, Bill or anything close to that, because his actual name was Trevor Harris. No, it was because when he cleaned the windows it never looked like he had cleaned the edges at all, just this round smudgy circle in the centre of the window pane. She assumed everyone must have known he was on the hobble, working for a bit of beer money. But for a blind, ageing window cleaner with a poor business model, he must have been doing ok as he turned up every two weeks. He never looked any cleaner than the time before and neither did his equipment but he was a plodder. She doubted he had ever filled in a tax return.

Years later he had passed away quietly in the armchair of his front room, with a couple of cans of his favourite brew at his side and his window cleaning gear at the side of the house, still dirty and still old. The thought of all this modern equipment with modern methods of payment would have blown his mind.

Both sisters were comfortable with the occasional silence, a moment in the day when they could get lost and reflect on whatever entered their minds in that moment. Following the constant stream of thoughts that flowed from one subject to the next. No conscious effort was ever needed, as if their minds were freewheeling down a hill with it's legs splayed apart with childish mindless pleasure.

11.30am

Carol had no idea what Janice had been thinking about. She guessed she must have been thinking about the life of squirrels or what pet rabbits do to pass the time. With the occasional S Club 7 tune echoing around her brain. And she was not surprised or let down with what Janice came out with next.

"I think tomorrow I'll buy myself a few spray cans," Janice announced.

Carol replied without hesitation, "Fair enough! Any particular reason why?"

Janice never failed to come up with some random statement or bit of information. Always something unrelated to anyone or anything happening in the real world or in the present moment. "Well you know that Banksy artist bloke?"

"Yeah, what about him?" and then something clicked in Carol's brain. "Oh no. Go on. But I can guess what you are going to say."

"Well you know he sprayed that garage with his artwork. His stuff sells for thousands. Well if I pick up a couple of spray cans and make those stencils I used to make while I was in college. I reckon I could do something like that, because that's all he does. I bet you he has a transit with cans of paint and stencils in the back, ready to vandalise somebody's private property. I could have a go and see if I can make a living out of it."

"Well, I can't see any flaws in your plan. Nothing whatsoever. Well, I can think of one thing."

"What's that? I know I'm not that stealthy, so that could be an issue. Or that neat for that matter. What's your one thing?" asked Janice.

"A catchy name. 'Banksy' is a catchy name, everyone knows a 'Banksy'. It's simple, easy to remember. What would your name be? And how would people find out what it was? 'Janice' is simple and easy, but not catchy. I can't imagine anyone pointing proudly at a 'Janice', and boasting to their mates, *'hey I bought one of those Janice's the other day'*."

"I'm sure I could come up with something given a bit of time. It's early days yet."

"And where would you put these works of art? I can't imagine anyone in our area being impressed by their property being vandalised by some middle aged yob with a stencil and a spraycan."

"True, I saw some kid tag somebody's house

once. This massive bloke came running from inside his house. Shouting and yelling. The kid scarpered around the corner into the dark. Unfortunately for the kid a number of things didn't go his way that evening, apart from getting seen."

"Like what?" asked Carol.

"Well firstly he spelled his name wrong. From his other work I think it was supposed to be *'Big Dog'* or something like that. Only he sprayed *'Big Bog'* on the wall. And the guy that owned the house was the local gang leader, who had cameras everywhere for security. And the poor kid had forgotten to put his hoodie up. Within hours he was caught after the gang leader had put the word out, he ended up in intensive-care for a few weeks."

"In that case both you and Banksy better be careful who's property you vandalise."

"On second thoughts," said Janice. "This is sounding like more hassle and stress than it's worth."

"Probably for the best. Sadly, you would be depriving the world of your talents. But better safe than sorry."

11.33am

"I didn't think we had left it at Mr Wallace's."

"That's ok. Shall we try the Carlton Hotel?"

"That's a great idea! They have a bar and a toilet."

"It's not even midday yet, it's a bit early for a pint, don't you think?"

"Excuse me," came a voice from behind, *"is this your bus pass?"*

"That's so kind of you, I can't take him any-where."

"She's my carer, I'm always losing stuff."

"You're welcome," said the young woman, as she handed the bus pass and carried on with her day.

"Do you think they'll remember me?"

"Do I think, the Mr and Mrs Thomas who run the Carlton Hotel, who had to give us a room for the night, after taking pity on you, who kindly fed us and allowing you a whiskey or two on the house, which resulted in you dancing and singing at the top of your voice and breaking a chair and

served us a hot cooked breakfast in the morning, remember you? I would have thought so."

"I did all of that?"

"That's the abridged version. I thanked Mr Thomas for their kindness and told Mrs Thomas she could have the goods compliments of the company."

"Wow, I didn't realise."

"Come on, let's see if they will still let us on the premises and see if she has come across our stuff."

11.35am

Carol pushed herself up a little more upright in her seat and swivelled to look behind her, first to her left and then to her right.

"What are you looking for?" asked Janice.

"Your pigeon friends. You have ten minutes until the moment of truth."

"Oh yeah, my guess was 11.45am. I am happy to make sure a thorough observation is made, so if they leave, I'll make a note of their departure and the direction they went."

"Yes, but where are they? I can't see them."

"They're on this side here, behind the bin. Don't worry I haven't taken my eye off them."

The 11.42am was due soon, only the odd passenger had come onto the platform.

"This is getting exciting now, they look like they are getting ready," said Janice keenly watching her subjects with interest.

Carol started doing her best David Attenborough impression, lowering her voice as she did her wildlife commentary. A more modern version of her unique David Bellamy impression, a celebrity from her much much younger days.

"The atmosphere is getting tense here on the platform. Two fine pigeon specimens strutting their stuff around in circles in readiness for take-off. As lunchtime approaches these two incredibly boring birds will need to find sustenance amongst the depths of Port Talbot's urban jungle. Braving the stench of the local inhabitants as they roam its Station Road savanna. Dodging mobility scooters that race through its centre. Hoping a feral child is careless with its Greggs pasty, crumbs falling as it tries to stuff as much fodder into its bloated face."

Just at that moment the two birds took flight.

"Oooh they're off! They're off!" Yelled Janice in sheer excitement. But her excitement soon turned into disappointment as the two birds found a perch underneath the overhead shelter. And each bird thought it a prudent time to preen underneath their wings and feathers.

"I thought that was the moment then," said Janice.

"I couldn't tell, can't say I noticed. Although that bloke on his phone down there, turned sharply to see what the commotion was. He looked really confused, looking to see what you were yelling at."

"He probably thinks you are my carer. I could get away with anything now," said Janice.

"People think I'm your carer at the best of times, let alone having a fit in the middle of the train station," replied Carol. "Just like when you had a go of those kids' Space Hoppers in the middle of the B&M store. You started off well, but you only really caused a scene when you lost confidence and fell off and crashed into the shelving."

"Oh I remember that, I couldn't stop laughing

because I got the Space Hopper stuck between my legs and I couldn't get up. I laughed so hard, a little bit of wee came out."

"Yeah, the staff weren't too impressed, as they had to reset the shelves. It was a good job there wasn't a passing whaler with a harpoon, he really would have thought his luck was in seeing your fat backside rolling in the aisle fighting with a Space Hopper."

"Yeah, not my most dignified moment. I didn't buy the Space Hopper either."

"Well we were both too embarrassed to spend any more time in there, especially since we were in the kids' section."

The bloke on the phone was still giving the odd glance towards the two strange women laughing at something, he was sure the younger must have some sort of mental health condition or something.

The 11.42am approached and came to a halt. The bloke on the phone continued his conversation as he got on the train.

11.45am, the time of reckoning.

"Right, any minute now," announced Janice, looking up to where the pigeons were perched. As she looked up, the two pigeons fluttered back to the platform floor. "Oop, oop, we have action. Go on, off you go."

Carol turned to look up at the clock, "11.46am, so your hopes of a 11.45am departure have well and truly gone up in flames."

"Well all isn't lost, it's not lunch time yet."

The two pigeons had now wandered closer to the platform's edge. The two women watched in silence. Carol had no real expectations, but Janice was inwardly getting more and more hopeful the longer time passed. And then without any notice Janice's pigeon took off, almost immediately followed by his girlfriend. Janice's mouth gaped open in amazement as the two pigeons arched around in flight. Carol shook her head in disbelief. And then both heads turned in unison as they tracked the birds as they headed towards Station Road in earnest. The two specks disappeared behind the buildings. Janice turned to look at Carol as if to say *'did you just see what I just saw'*. Carol's gaze was still fixed in the direction of the departed birds, her reaction was a bit delayed. Janice slowly pulled out her phone from her pocket.

"Well I must admit I really didn't expect that. I was happy to play along, but really wasn't expecting them to do that at that moment. Did you notice how they arched around in a sweeping motion." Janice had stopped listening. Carol became suddenly aware she wasn't getting any kind of response and out of the corner of her eye could see something odd going on.

She turned to look. "What on earth are you doing?"

Janice had risen off her seat and was now doing some sort of weird victory dance "Naa na, na na naaa, na." Both index fingers pointing in the air, alternating her arms up and down. "Call me the pigeon whisperer, call me the queen of the birds, call me Janice Doolittle, she talks to the animals, come on!"

"You do realise you are on CCTV," said Carol nodding towards the camera angled in their direction. "If we end up on YouTube or going viral on any social media I'll throttle you, you know I don't trust Bill."

"Oh Bill's harmless, he's probably having a

good giggle himself. It'll brighten up his secu-rity shift. Anyway, that was amazing, that's go-ing straight on my report to the RSPB. I'll need to clear my diary for when they come looking to interview me. I'll probably end up on Coun-tryfile too, once word gets around."

"I think you are getting a little ahead of yourself. You'll probably get a polite thank you for your diligent observations, before getting archived or binned along with the bird watch-ing communities emails. Don't get me wrong, I hope you get on the telly. I mean, I didn't think they would fly away as predicted, so why should I be correct in thinking you won't get on the telly with Kate Humble, stranger things have happened."

"Exactly, I'd better get myself a check pat-terned top, wellies and one of those posh bodywarmer jacket things, which everyone has started calling a fancy name."

"A gilet."

"That's them a gilet, probably bright red to look the part next to Kate."

"You are forgetting one thing," said Carol.

"What?"

"We're in the middle of a town and not in the countryside. There isn't a hay bale to sit on for miles."

"Well we could stage that. I'm sure we could rustle up some goats and lambs too, to have in the background to make things look authentic. Or if we talk nicely to one of the farmers not too far away, and tempt them with meeting Kate Humble, that would definitely work. Alternatively, they could do a segment on Port Talbot's urban wildlife, headed by yours truly."

"Urban wildlife? On a train station platform? A couple of pigeons, countless gulls and if you are particularly lucky the odd rat running the tracks. I can't see that happening," observed Carol.

"It's work in progress, what can I say? And I'll discuss it with the research team when we have our production meeting."

"Did you bring any cold water?"

"No, why?" asked Janice.

"It's got quite warm now and I could do with something cold."

"I tell you what, I'll see if Pam or Bill have anything," Janice got up and started to make her way down the platform. "Do you want anything else while I'm gone?"

"I don't think so. I've got stuff to eat, I just need something cold to drink."

"Righto. While I'm with Pam and Bill, I'll mentally prepare them for my upcoming TV fame and reassure them that nothing will change and I'll remain the down to earth charismatic Janice they've always known." said Janice.

"That's really thoughtful of you, well done."

Carol took this opportunity to enjoy some peace. Dull and boring were very much what was required right now. Janice would be back soon and dull and boring would swiftly evaporate into the ether.

She leaned back, letting her whole body relax into the seat. It had gone midday and the temperature was much higher than forecast. At times like these she really enjoyed being in the moment. The heat of the sun had warmed the air sufficiently to feel like she was being warmed by an open fire. She closed her eyes and let the warmth wash over her. The traffic had become an ambient noise in the background. As she felt any remaining tension melt away, the cry of the seagulls became more distinct and the odd tinkering noises from some distant workshop could also be heard as someone hammered some metalwork. The breeze felt lovely against her face.

12.10pm

No passengers as yet were waiting for the 12.12pm train.

Carol opened her eyes. She winced and almost immediately closed them again. And then tried again slowly. The sunlight was very bright and her eyes had been closed long enough for them to need time to readjust. She assumed she must have dozed off for a few moments, losing consciousness in the heat.

As her eyes refocused she caught sight of the 12.12pm arriving. It pulled into the station, It waited a short while before revving the engines to pull away. As the rear engine passed Carol. A familiar figure came into view carrying two mugs and a bottle under each arm. And a massive smile on her face, a face that looked like it was dying to report on what she had just been up to.

"All I wanted was a cold drink. Why have you got two mugs of whatever?"

"I have got two cold drinks. Take this." She handed Carol one of the mugs.

"Do you expect me to drink out of one of those bottles after they have been under your armpits? And what is in this mug, it looks nice, but what is it?"

"Oh don't worry, I had a shower this morning and they are still cold. I haven't long got them out of the fridge and it's cappuccino in the mug. They are awesome, have a taste."

"Ok, I feel I need more of an explanation. What fridge? and where did you get two mugs? and how did you fill them with cappuccino?"

"Right well, I saw Pam and she took me into the office-cum-staffroom. Bill was sat in front of the CCTV monitors. He said he was in stitches watching me doing my dance, but his phone had decided to update its software at the same time, so he couldn't record, he was gutted. And you were right he would have put me on social media. I said you'd kill him if he put you on there. You should see his phone, it's one of those double screen jobbies, it's fancy, you wouldn't like it. Anyway Pam grabbed me two bottles from the fridge for us, she said just pop by anytime we wanted one. And then, and then..."

"Woe, slow down, take a breath, you'll hyperventilate if you carry on," warned Carol.

"Don't interrupt I'm getting to the best bit, you'll like this. As Bill was showing me his phone, Pam walked over to this new fancy coffee machine and pressed a button and made herself this fancy coffee. It was pretty hefty, the real deal. It has all the bells and whistles. If you wanted a mocha, a flat white, an americano, hot chocolate and even just frothy milk, it could do it for you. So I got us two cappuccinos, she said we could pop the mugs back later. What do you think?"

Carol took a sip, savoured the taste, "Yes it's nice, makes a nice change."

"Doesn't it?! It's not cheap stuff. I said I'll give her some money towards it so they can get some more."

"How come they have it in the first place?

I can't imagine British Rail supplies fancy machines to all their staff."

"It was left unclaimed in lost and found. Brand new, can you believe that."

"Fair enough."

"What's the difference between a flat white and a cappuccino? Do you know?" asked Janice.

"Cappuccino has one espresso shot with two parts milk froth and flat white has a double shot espresso with a smoother froth, apparently it's all to do with how the milk is prepared. Along those lines anyway."

"That was quick and comprehensive. So what's a latte?"

"Why don't you go down to Costa Coffee and ask?"

"Hey, I just got you a cappuccino. I only asked."

"Sorry, it's lovely. A latte is completely milk, but you are better off asking Google." Carol wiped her cold bottle of water on her top to remove any armpit residue. Unscrewed the lid and took a sip of water. "Did you explain why you were dancing to Bill?"

"Oh yeah. I did tell him why I was dancing,

he gave me a high five. He said he hadn't really paid attention to the pigeons before, but he would from now on and let me know if it's a regular occurrence. He also said his niece does a lot of bird watching and does the *'Big Garden Birdwatch'* every year. She loves all that, he said we should sign up. Pam also said there was an old woman that feeds the birds everyday on the corner of Forge Road. So that might have something to do with it. I might leave that bit out of my report, it might detract from my discovery."

Carol smiled, "Yeah probably best leave that bit out, I can't imagine Kate Humble being impressed by that."

Janice drained her mug. "Well I really enjoyed that. Oh yes, I did mention Kate and my future stardom. They felt suitably reassured after I said I wouldn't let it change me."

Carol continued to take her time drinking her drink as they watched some of the traffic pass by. A massive articulated lorry pulled up at the lights. Along its side was a huge picture of a hot, mouth watering pie, its contents of meat and gravy spilling out in a tantalising way.

"I'd like to think I'm immune to advertising,

but that pie really makes me feel like getting one," said Carol.

"Oh I know, we could pop over to the chip shop and get one on the way home."

"That would be nice, good idea. As regards advertising, you are an advertising agent's dream, you'd buy anything. *'New and original knicker warmers out now! Fully equipped with wifi and bluetooth. Use the knicker warmer app on your phone and experience the thrill of a warm bum in the dead of winter. Different heat settings to suit your rear's needs. Fifty percent off when you refer a friend, buy one get one free. Out now, don't miss out'.* You'd be straight on the internet getting yours."

"Yes that's true," said Janice. "I can't help it. They are not allowed to lie on adverts so I think it's all true. They are so convincing and they show me stuff I didn't know I needed. And you are right, I am an advertiser's dream. I've spent a fortune on junk, stuff that didn't live up to expectations."

"Didn't you buy a chicken harness and leash off Amazon?"

"Yes I still got it somewhere."

"Why did you buy it? We don't have any chickens let alone one you could take for a walk."

"Well, I saw an article about chickens becoming more popular as pets. And was so inspired by it, I bought the harness and leash in readiness for my new pet chicken. I realised the next morning clearing my wine bottle and glass away that I realised that a chicken isn't just for Christmas and I would neither have the time or patience to look after it."

"And you didn't think to return it? But decided to clutter up the house with it."

"You never know, it might come in handy. We may have a friend who suddenly needs to walk their chicken immediately. And when that knock on the door comes, we will be ready and able to help."

"I stand corrected. It isn't clutter, it's a precious resource in the event of a real life emergency. Anyway, where did you see those knicker warmers?" asked Janice.

"I didn't, I made them up."

"I'm going to search for a pair on the interweb right now."

12.30pm

"On a different, more relevant subject, did you pack yourself food for lunch?" asked Carol.

"I did! I had tortilla wraps left over from last night. I made a couple of healthy and non healthy ones," said Janice.

"Go on."

"Okay so the healthy ones are loaded with rocket, spinach, olives, feta cheese and some sesame seeds. And the non healthy ones are loaded with M&Ms and Nutella spread."

"Your face totally lit up when you said Nutella, just then," said Carol

"Well we weren't allowed it when we were young were we? Remember when we went to the shops with Mam? She flat refused to buy it, that and Sugar Puffs."

"Yes. And I remember you having a tizzy fit in the aisle because she made you put it back. You were not happy."

"Well I was a kid. I remember asking her why she wouldn't buy Crunchynut Cornflakes. Can you remember what she used to say?"

"Oh yes. She would say *'It's because you eat it all,'*" Carol said, smiling to herself wistfully.

Janice continued, "I understand now obviously, but I remember being totally confused by that. She was forever trying to get us to eat all our breakfast. Porridge just didn't cut it, that and Weetabix. And how could they when we knew Crunchynut Cornflakes and Sugar Puffs were in the world or the ultimate as far as I was concerned, Frosties!"

"I tried making the porridge and Weetabix a bit more interesting by either mixing them together or by adding plain Cornflakes for a bit of crunch. But you have always had a sweeter tooth than me. You were a kleptomaniac when it came to getting your sugar fix."

"What do you mean? I don't remember that."

"No I don't suppose you do. You were only three years old and you were sat in the supermarket's trolley toddler seat. When Mam wasn't looking you grabbed a pack of bubble-gum. It was only as she was walking us away from the shop she realised you were stuffing your face with a whole packet of bubble-gum. Not just that, but they were a stolen packet of bubble-gum. She was mortified and I remember she took us back inside to pay for them. She kept a close eye on you from then on, and frisked you before we left any shop for stolen goods."

"No, I don't remember that. I do remember having a fetish for bubble-gum. I had to have my mouth washed out with soap and water after I picked up some of the pavement and put it in my mouth. She was horrified and scrubbed my mouth out. That I do remember, I'm sure I still have chunks of Imperial Leather soap in my mouth somewhere."

"So apart from your wraps, did you pack anything else?"

"I did bring some of that cake we had in the kitchen. But that's mainly it, oh and a can of Coke, but I was saving that until a little later. Did you pack yours before I got out of bed?"

"I did, I made myself some jam and cheese sandwiches. And I packed some crisps too. I also have some herbal teas. I didn't know what I wanted so I brought several different bags."

"Very nice!" approved Janice.

A few moments later a father and son emerged onto the platform. The little boy who was around eight or nine years old caught Janice's eye. He looked very excited, he wore a blue t-shirt. "Look at that little boy's hair."

"What about it?"

"Well it's gorgeous. I love the way it's not quite shoulder length, it's so blonde and curly. When little boys have hair like that, I always assume his parents are really laid back people. Not so permissive to let him do absolutely whatever he likes but just enough so he can express himself. Or if he wants to try an activity like climbing, skate-boarding or surfing they will make sure he is able to have a proper go at it. And that they are outdoorsy people, always doing some walk up in the Brecon Beacons somewhere, and they travel in a VW camper."

"I know what you mean. He's posher than we were at that age, not that we were posh, but he's innocent enough not to know any different or to know that he's more privileged than we were. He does look excited."

The little boy had spotted the freight train coming down the tracks pulling its load.

"Oh he's seen this freight train coming," said Carol.

The train was moving at a steady pace as it approached the station and was obviously passing straight through. The boy started jumping up and down waving frantically at the train.

"Oh love him. He's trying to get the attention of the driver. I hope the driver waves back, I used to love that when I was younger," said Janice.

The driver had noticed the little boy and the little boy was going to get more than just a wave. The train drew much closer and the boy could now see the driver clearly in the cabin. He waved much harder and vigorously. As he did the driver honked the train's horn and the little boy almost wet himself in excitement. He carried on frantically waving as the train passed, looking back at his dad and then back at the train. The train was carrying carriages of timber and they just kept coming one after the other.

"That is the best," said Janice loudly. "That's going to make that little boy's day. He is going to be buzzing. To get a honk off a train is just the best."

The little boy was still jumping in excitement.

He turned around and as he caught sight of Janice and Carol, Janice stuck two thumbs up and mouthed *'Awesome'*. The little boy saw her and stuck his thumbs up back at her. His dad was just smiling at his little boy, he also smiled at Janice in acknowledgement.

Carol raised her voice and said, "That is so refreshing, to see a little boy like that getting so excited over the train." As she did the last of the carriages passed them by and off into the distance. Then father and son left the platform.

12.35pm

Meanwhile, having reached the ice-cream parlour, post Carlton Hotel visit.

"I think Mrs Thomas must like you, to still give you a complimentary coffee and a use of her loo."

"What woman could resist this face."

"I wouldn't know. But since you've been a good boy I will let you choose your own ice-cream today? What do you want?"

"Looking at the menu, I'm not sure whether

to have the Amaretto, Coppa Amarena or a Knickerbockerglory."

"We'll need to pop into the Marina before heading home. So I would appreciate it, if you didn't spend too long choosing."

"So much ice-cream, so little time."

"Are we talking about just now, or how long you've got left on your remaining lifespan?"

"I'm in my prime I'll have you know."

"Have you made your mind up?"

"I'll have the Gelato Affogato please."

"Good choice. I'll text Jenny to meet us at the Marina to check her boat."

12.45pm

The next train wasn't due until 01.17pm.

"Are you going to put the one o'clock news on?" asked Carol.

"Why would I?"

"Well you said earlier this morning Mr Stresshead could have been reporting a drugs cartel bust."

"Oh yes," said Janice, smiling. "We could try, I'll tell my phone to remind me." She pulled out her phone and pressed a key to activate the phone assistant. "Set a reminder for 1pm to watch..."

"Ok, what time would you like the reminder," interrupted the assistant.

"Goodness me, I hate it when she does that."

"Sorry, I didn't quite catch that. What time would you like to set your reminder?"

"One," said Janice.

"Is that one in the morning or one in the afternoon?"

"This afternoon."

"Reminder is set for 1pm. What would you like me to remind you to do?"

"To watch the news!" This time much louder and angrier than before. Revealing her ever increasing frustration. "I said that at the beginning."

"Okay, I will remind you to watch the news at 1pm."

"It'll be 1pm by the time you have set the reminder. I don't know why you bother," said Carol.

"Well it's supposed to be able to help, it can be really useful."

"Yes, but when she doesn't understand you, I can see you physically getting frustrated. Your face distorts in an angry little way and it gives away that your blood-pressure is starting to soar. You raise your voice and eventually start shouting at it. And the more she messes up, the quicker you go from calm zero to apoplectic."

"Yes I know, we have this sort of love-hate relationship."

"You do, with her you mean. She has no idea she's in a relationship with you. In fact I doubt she's even aware she's upsetting you in any way."

"I really don't know how I got here. Years ago I was over the moon just to have a pocket organiser. Now I'm talking and shouting at the technology. I can't believe I call her by her name, I've even bought into the idea of her having a gender by calling *it* a *her*. And then I get annoyed when she doesn't do what I want her to do."

"I find the same thing with you. And do you know what the scary thing is?" asked Carol.

"What?"

"There's no going back. You have started

down a slippery slope, you've fallen into the venus flytrap of the technology world. Apps, socials, A.I, online banking, smart light bulbs, where will it stop? The answer. Nobody knows! Soon Asimov's three laws will become a reality and we won't be able to wipe our bums without some sort of digital finger getting involved. And the only way out will be smashing it all with a hammer," said Carol.

"You are depressing me now. I'm going to eat a wrap to comfort myself followed by my heavily loaded sugar fix wraps and hopefully I'll be on such a sugar rush I'll forget about what you just said. And continue in blissful blind ignorance." Janice pulled out her backpack and delved in, in search for her wraps.

"I think I'll join you." Carol pulled out her sandwiches and crisps.

Janice had her wraps in a tupperware box. She took out a wrap and put the lid back on the box and popped it on the floor, and took a bite out of the wrap. Carol had placed her sand-wiches in a sandwich bag, designed for such an occasion. She pulled out a teatowel, placed it over her lap and then placed the sandwiches on the teatowel. She took one and bit off one of the corners. She then opened her crisps and then lifted off the top of the sandwich and filled it with the crisps. She bit down on the loaded sandwich.

"That is such a satisfying feeling. I love sandwiches stuffed with crisps," said Janice.

Carol's mouth was full of sandwich. "Mmhmm", was the best she could respond with.

"I will interpret that as a *'yes Janice, I totally agree. The soft texture of the multigrain buttery slices, followed by the satisfying crunchiness of the crisps is delicious. Usually they are best con-sumed by filling your mouth up with as much as will possibly fit into the considerable hole in your face and chewing gently.'* I think that's what you were trying to get across."

Carol, mouth now empty, replied, "I couldn't have put that better myself. Although I did notice you wasted no time wolfing down your wrap, you are allowed to chew before swallow-ing you know. I threw a fish into the mouth of a sealion once at a wildlife park, it wasn't as quick as you swallowing it. If you hand me one of your wraps, I would be happy to do the same for you, it might be just as easy. "

"That's very kind of you. I tell you what, when I eat the other half I will masticate profusely, just to make you happy."

"Thank you."

Once again both fell silent as they enjoyed their food and the warm air that surrounded them.

1pm

Just a couple of minutes later, their blissful lunch was rudely interrupted by an alarm, followed by, "this is a reminder to watch the one o'clock news, this is a reminder to watch the one o'clock news."

"Well that ruined the moment," said Carol.

"Shut up, shut up! Stop! Alright I got it," Janice frantically turned off her phone assistant and clicked on BBC Iplayer and turned on the news.

"Good afternoon, this is the BBC news at one o'clock, the headlines this afternoon..." came the voice from the phone.

"That's Reeta Chalrabarti, I like her," said Janice. Reeta read each headline in turn.

"No mention of any South Wales drug bust. It was a nice idea though. Maybe check the regional news tonight, you never know, they may have it ready for this evening."

"I'll see how I feel later. I've recorded some programmes, so I'll probably catch up later. Shall I turn this off now?" asked Janice, holding up her phone.

"Yes it's grim, it's all bad news. I don't know how those presenters keep it together. I'd either be balling my eyes out or giving out my own opinion and insulting the latest political leader as they produce their latest scandal. I don't think I could cope with that much responsibility live on telly. I'd get the sack within minutes," said Carol.

"That's true. You nearly got kicked out of Wetherspoons after expressing your opinion to the staff in a less than friendly way about the breakfast. That was a day I'd rather forget. I could only imagine what you'd say let loose on live television. The BBC would definitely sack you, but I bet you ITV would give you your own show," said Janice.

"Hey that's true, there must be something Ant and Dec aren't doing."

"The Voice," Janice said immediately, like some sort of reflex action, "they are not on there. You could be the female judge. And you would be sat between Will.I.Am and our gorgeous Tom."

"Yes! That would be brilliant. I would be great as a coach. How do I apply for that job? Or should I ring ITV directly and tell them I'm available? That's probably why they haven't approached me already, they don't know I'm available." said Carol.

"Get on it! You'll be spinning your chair with the best of them before you know it."

1.15pm

A number of people had all arrived on the platform, which was a very good indicator the next train was about to arrive. One business man had a small rucksack. He wasn't wearing a tie and had his shirt top button undone allowing his collar free. He was also carrying his suit jacket over his arm with a coffee in his other hand. He looked at his watch and then up at the arrivals screen, as if to double check his watch matched the platform time.

Another couple looked like they were going away for the weekend, as they pulled their flight bags noisily down the platform. They were in deep conversation as the train arrived.

As the train stopped the business man tried to open the door. He pulled the handle but managed to spill some hot coffee on his fingers and then onto his shirt.

"Oh that's going to hurt," said Janice.

"He's got it on his shirt too. He looks like he's going to a business meeting or some sort of working lunch to discuss things with col-leagues. I would not be happy turning up with a massive coffee stain on my shirt."

"And he's going to have to put up with that for the day, 'cause coffee doesn't wipe down that easily."

"I bet you he goes on golfing weekends too."

"With the lads," said Janice.

"Yes, but he'll call it networking."

"Where do you think the couple were going? They looked really trendy in their skinny jeans and soft shoes. I couldn't wear skinny jeans like that, no matter how much I pushed and shoved. These thighs and these calves ain't getting into them."

"Nor me. I had a friend who tried getting into a pair of them once. They were evidently a size too small as they were, but she was convinced they were the right size."

"Who was that?" asked Janice.

"Denise. Do you know her?"

"Can't say I do."

"Well anyway, we were round her house and she had been shopping and bought these skinny jeans. She was smaller than me, but that still wasn't going to be of any help. She said they were slightly elasticated and would stretch a little. So she got them up her legs so far and then they just wouldn't go any further up," said Carol.

"What happened?"

"Physics! There was still too much of her to fit into them. But she was adamant they were the correct size and she had heard that talc would help. So she still kept the jeans on, as she bunny hopped into the bathroom for the talc. She poured it around her legs and tried again to squeeze into them, but still nothing. So rather than give in, she just pulled harder. And all of a sudden the jeans split and her hands slipped as she fell backwards into the bath, whacking on the shower at the same time. She got absolutely soaked and the talc congealed all around her legs. And it didn't help that she hadn't shaved her legs either, so the talc had lots to cling to."

"And what did you do while this was all going on?" asked Janice.

"Well as she didn't listen to my advice and ignored my suggestion to get a bigger size and continued to ignore me as I told her she should maybe not pull so hard and give up, I did what any good friend would do. I totally left her floundering in the bath to get soaked and I wet myself laughing from a safe distance."

"Quite right. And do you ever see this Denise?"

"I haven't seen her in a long while. The last time we spoke she was making plans to run a surf school in Cornwall somewhere, so I assume she's down there somewhere, living the dream," said Carol.

"I think most people would have a laugh watching me put my socks on these days let alone skinny jeans," said Janice. "When did putting socks on become so hard, do you find that?"

"Yep, socks, tights, walking boots, anything with a lace. If I have to bend down for any reason, and need to use all that energy, I plan my trip and see if there is anything else that needs doing while I'm down there. If my nails need cutting, If there's anything on the floor that needs picked up or if it needs cleaning."

"Paint the skirting boards." suggested Janice.

"Paint the skirting boards, yes, and just about anything else I can find," said Carol.

"I've started to make involuntary noises now. A noise if I have to go down to my foot or if I'm sitting, a noise as I raise my foot, and then get the sock on the first part of my foot. Then a noise as I pull the sock up. And the worrying thing is that I don't know when all this started. How did I go from slip my sock on easily, slip my sock on easily, and then what seems to be the next day, risking injury and A&E with every sock I wrestle with."

"I make a noise every time I get up or sit down on a comfortable chair," said Carol.

"I've noticed that. I'm not quite there yet. But it's good to be ahead of the game and know what to expect next."

"So just to be clear, skinny jeans are off any present list?" asked Carol.

"That is correct. Anything with an elasticated waste band would be most welcome," agreed Janice.

A middle aged couple had came onto the platform. They placed their bags on the seats and the woman started rifling through one of them searching for something. The man started to set up a tripod that came to almost head height. And then fixed his phone to it and promptly removed it again.

"What is this pair up to?" asked Carol.

"Trainspotters."

"How can you tell?"

"Well I saw a similar couple last week doing the same thing, only they had a young child with them," said Janice.

"Oh yeah, I remember. I don't think I've seen this couple before."

They both watched the trainspotting couple as they got themselves ready. The woman had found what she was looking for, her notepad and pen. She opened up the notepad to the correct page. She also pulled out a sandwich, which she held in her mouth as she scribbled a few notes in her pad. The man had sat down, having got himself ready.

"I'm going to go over and have a chat with them, I've not spoken to any of the spotters that come here in a while," announced Janice.

"What are you going to talk to them about?"

"Trainspotting obviously."

Janice made her way over to the couple, who now seemed more settled. She gave a warm smile as she approached them.

"Hello, how are you guys?"

"Oh hello, we're fine thank you," said the woman.

"I have to ask, are you guys trainspotting today?"

"We are, how could you tell?" she said smiling.

"Well, my sister and I spend a lot of time here, so we recognise the signs. My name is Janice by the way."

"Oh I'm Susan and this is my husband Geoff. We love it, it's not everyone's cup of tea but we really enjoy it."

"I've never really asked what you guys actually do, I guess it's pretty much self explanatory."

"Yes, it's exactly as the name implies. But it's not just left to chance, we have an itinerary," she said, raising her notepad. "Me and Geoff know what trains are coming through and when. So we have a list of the train numbers, here, see," she said showing her a well organised sheet of paper, "these numbers are on the front of the trains, today we're also expecting a steam train coming through, so that'll be a real treat to add to the collection."

"Oh wow, that'll be a treat for us too. Carol, my sister loves steam engines. She's a real Fred Dibnah fan. So she'll be really over the moon to see one of those. Is it a special one? If you know what I mean?"

"Yeah I know what you mean. Yes it's actually

a pair of Black Five steam engines, pulling carriages with tourists. 45407 and 44871." said Susan without looking at her notes.

"And these numbers are on the trains?"

"Yes they are the numbers of each engine. When your usual trains come through they will also have a number on the front, you probably wouldn't have paid attention to it. But these engines are lush, they have a lovely livery. They'll blow you away when they come past. Seeing them at full chuff up close is very impressive."

"I know what you mean. There's something about the smell and the noise that revives a life long ago. I would have loved to have seen this area as it was a hundred years or so back. The railway used to go right up the valley there. I've only seen a few rare pics myself," said Janice.

Geoff had poured himself a coffee and sipped it as Janice and Susan discussed the trainspotting itinerary.

Janice looked down to Geoff. "You alright there Geoff, do you love the steam train scene too?"

Before Geoff could open his mouth to

answer, Susan replied for him, "Oh he loves it. Don't you Geoff?" Geoff realising he wasn't going to get a word in, just smiled and nodded. As Susan looked back at Janice, he caught Janice's eye, and rolled his eyes back, and without saying a word to each other, both understood that Susan would be the designated talker for the duration. "Are you waiting for the 01.42 train?"

"No, my sister and I come down twice a week and simply sit on the platform and watch the world go by. We've done it for a while, so that's what we're up to today. When is the steam train coming?" No answer came as Susan's attention was diverted up track.

The 1.42pm train was on time and this hadn't escaped Susan's notice.

Susan slapped Geoff on the shoulder and pointed the train out. "Here comes the first one." Geoff got up and attached his phone to the tripod and aimed it in the direction of the train and pressed record. All three were now looking down the track towards the oncoming train.

"Have you got a list of trains you're waiting for? How long do you trainspot for in a day?"

"Today, we will be here until the steam train comes and goes. But we did take the time to make a list of the trains we could expect as a bit of a bonus. So we'll be making a note of those and filming them as we wait."

The train entered the station, the train number on the cabin could now be clearly seen.

"175 107 Geoff," said Susan as she ticked it off her list and made a note.

Geoff focused in on the cabin with the camera as it passed, but kept filming as the carriages followed.

Janice didn't want to interrupt the moment as both Geoff and Susan were fully focused on the task at hand. After all, this was one of the reasons they were here. She waited until the train was departing before asking anything else.

"Did you get that Geoff?"

Geoff replayed the footage and adjusted his glasses to see if all was ok. "Yep", he said after careful consideration.

"Do you know the type of engine that was too as well as the number?" asked Janice.

"A 1 V50," said Geoff without hesitation.

"That was quick, you definitely know your

trains. Not that I can verify that," she said smiling.

"Oh yes, Geoff knows his stuff. I got him a train simulator for the PC and hooked it up to the big screen. He was in his element."

"Wow, have you done this route Geoff?"

"Oh he has," said Susan. "When did you do this route love?"

"Last January," said Geoff, giving the information asked for. He knew any additional information would be superfluous. And Susan would interrupt anyway.

"I made sure he packed his bag before starting. Made sure he had his phone, wallet, keys, food etc. you know all the essential stuff. It would have been a disaster if he had started from Milford Haven and didn't have everything, I mean this is stop number 12 and he would have to wait quite a while before leaving his post."

"So when you say a simulator, he doesn't just pause for a pee break on a route, he actually sits and does the journey?"

"Do it properly or not at all I say. We have a friend who does the same with his aeroplane simulator. He does London to New York non stop."

"What's your longest journey Geoff?" asked Janice. Geoff looked up to see if it was worth opening his mouth. And it wasn't.

"The 'Canadian Mountain Passes' is his longest. But we've ordered a Scotrail simulator which should be epic. Plus an extension pack. We love doing the long haulage routes"

"Do you sit with him then on these journeys?"

"Absolutely, I can't let him have all the fun by himself."

"No, I don't suppose you can. So you have to pack a bag too then?"

"Oh yes."

"Do you do any of the driving?"

"Sometimes, but Geoff mainly does it."

"Do you ever get a little bored waiting for the next train?"

"Oh no, there's a whole network of us trainspotters all over the socials. So between trains we're usually on our phones catching up with the latest videos and pics."

Janice was now actually getting a bit bored

and decided it may be best leave Susan and Geoff concentrate.

"Well it's great getting to know you guys, I'll leave you guys to it. Thanks for letting me know about the steam train."

"No problem. We'll pop the footage on You-Tube later. If you want to look us up, we're 'G&S trainspotters network'."

"Great stuff. See you later Geoff."

Geoff saluted his coffee in Janice's direction and Janice made her way back to Carol.

"You were there a while. If you'd been there any longer I would have had to get you an anorak," said Carol.

"Oh I know, but seeing Susan and Geoff's enthusiasm was infectious at first, but as I asked more questions the deeper it got more and more tedious and then I could feel myself zoning out, so I thought it best to leave before it turned into me looking bored out of my skull."

"Very Wise."

"But, they did tell me a steam train would be coming through here today."

"Did they say what time?"

"Ah, no, but I'm not going back over there

to ask now. Although they did say we could catch up on YouTube, once they've uploaded the footage. So we could watch it later if we've left by the time it comes through."

"Woop woop. Well let's hope we see it in person then. I would be embarrassed if my search history revealed I had been looking for trainspotters on YouTube. If parental guidance options included that, I would tick the box immediately."

"Right I need some cake and a sugar filled can of Coke to counteract the soporific trainspotting," said Janice.

"Too right, live life on the edge I say. Well the edge of diabetes as far as you're concerned. What cake do you have?"

"Carrot. The one we started yesterday but never finished."

"That's still really sweet, despite involving a carrot," said Carol.

"I did actually look up the symptoms of diabetes the other day," said Janice.

"And what did you learn?"

"Well the symptoms were moodiness, tiredness, nausea and headaches. But that could also mean I'm pregnant, have the flu or chronic fatigue. So I was none the wiser."

"That'll teach you for going to Dr. Google."

"It was useful for some stuff, but yeah, as soon as I Google any illness I'm sure I have it within seconds. Do you remember Deirdre who worked in the Chemist on Station Road?"

"Unibrow Deirdre? Thick glasses? Moustache?" asked Carol.

"That's the one. Well that was the worst job for her, well maybe for her son at least."

"Why was that?"

"Every time her son came down with a mild cold or stomach ache, she couldn't leave it at that, it was always something more serious. The longer she worked in the pharmacists the more illnesses she learnt about. And remember this was before Dr. Google. And the more illnesses she was introduced to, then her son would be diagnosed with whatever the latest one she came across."

"Poor kid."

"It's a good job she definitely knew he was a boy, otherwise he would have had a whole load of other issues if he was a girl," said Janice.

"Does she still work there?"

"Well she did, right up until she died suddenly."

"What do you mean suddenly? What happened?"

Janice started to laugh, "I shouldn't laugh, but one of those tall medicine cabinets, you know the ones? The ones right behind the till, it fell on top of her and killed her on the spot. Apparently they had been recently installed and hadn't been fixed to the wall properly."

"That is not how I imagined she wanted to go."

"No, I guess not. Apparently the old lady she was serving nearly had a heart attack from the shock."

"I bet she was traumatised too," said Carol.

"Yes I bet. If you had to go suddenly, how would you like to go?"

"I wouldn't, I was hoping to live to a ripe old age and pass away in my sleep face down with my knees bent and bum in the air, dressed as a Stormtrooper, ready for when the undertakers come to take me away. And I would hope the rigamortis would have set me in that position, so when everyone came to see me at the chapel of rest, they would see me still in that pose, in the same outfit, with one single rose placed between my bum cheeks. I have never given any thought to a sudden scenario. You got me thinking now. Give me five minutes. What about you?"

"I have given this one a little thought. If, given the choice, I would like to die eating M&M's, wearing a hippo onesie. I would be fed them while in the arms of Chris Hemsworth, as we sat watching the sunset on some Caribbean island. I wouldn't die of M&M overdose, but just of sheer happiness. And as I slipped away, I would let off a mild but steady fart as my last breath."

"That is very specific, considering you've given that *little thought*. I don't know how I would want to go, I'll have to come back to you on that one."

1.55pm

Susan and Geoff were now settled on their

seats and thumbing their phones through the latest socials.

While Carol and Janice had been talking, Janice had pulled out her cake and Coke. The cake was in a tupperware box and she had also put a little fork in with it. She popped the Coke on the seat beside her and started to make her way through her cake.

"I know it's probably the sugar and whatnot, but this cake tastes so good. Maybe it's because I haven't had to pay an extortionate amount from a coffee shop or I'm eating it here. Whatever it is, it tastes amazing and makes me so happy. What is the food that makes you happy? You know, that meal or morsel that takes you to that happy place."

"Well that's a bit easier for me to answer. Chicken curry from the chip shop with half'n'half, half chips and half rice. Doused in salt and vinegar. And the best place I've ever had it from, is from Margam Fish Bar, sat in my old Vauxhall Nova. But realistically I could eat it anywhere."

"That sounds good, I personally couldn't rank it higher than my carrot cake, but it's not far off," said Janice picking up her Coke, having polished off her cake. She pulled the ring to open it and it made a satisfying 'Psst' sound. She brought it to her lips and took a sip. "Oh no."

"What?"

"Warm Coke. It's so warm today. I didn't account for that when I put it in my bag. I'll push on through though. I am not going to give up the sugar rush just because the temperature isn't right."

"I wouldn't expect you to, you are such a trooper. In further news, I have given your question about dying suddenly some thought and I have an answer of sorts. I'm not sure you'll be happy with it, but I do have one"

"Go on."

"I don't think I could be as specific as you. However, my way would be sudden. If given the choice I would like it to be a surprise."

"Hey? A surprise?"

"Yes, how can I put it? An unexpected explosion for instance. A sudden fall from such a height as to be aware that I was falling and know I was about to die, but I wouldn't want to fall so long that would allow me to dwell on it. And whichever way I went, I would like it to be painless. You know I wouldn't want it to be slow and agonising, like drowning or being chewed on by a lion."

"Well that's fair enough. Maybe the explosion could happen in a pub. A beer barrel erupts and you watch it come towards you and it hits you square in the head and you fall off the table you were dancing on."

"Yes, that sort of thing. In a brewery or an ice-cream factory."

"Oh an ice-cream factory, now that's a fantastic place for a surprise demise. Falling from a great height into a vat of deluxe salted caramel and having the mother of all brain freezes," said Janice.

"I said no pain. I can't deal with normal ice-cream brain freeze," reminded Carol.

"Oh yeah. Still it would be a legendary way to go. We could scoop you out, keep you frozen and bury you in a giant plastic container to complete the effect."

"Like Port Talbot's equivalent of Han Solo being carbon frozen, only with ice-cream, I really like that idea, well sort of, apart from the me being dead bit."

2.05pm.

A group of youngsters emerged onto the platform. Giggling and laughing.

"That's nice," said Janice.

"What is?"

"Seeing youngsters laughing like that. Every time I walk through town these days, lots of the youngsters I pass look grumpy or look like they are up to no good, whether they are or not."

One of the girls had a selfie stick and had everyone in a huddle for a group photo, with the usual peace sign, two fingers held up and an obligatory tongue was also stuck out.

"It's a good job we didn't have selfie sticks when we were young. Dad would definitely have had us in a huddle every two minutes on whatever holiday we were on," said Carol.

"Do you remember he bought a tripod for his camera one time. He had a timer on the camera, and the only way you knew it had taken the photo was waiting for the shutter to go off."

"Oh yeah, I'd forgotten about that. We had to stay stiff, with massive grins on our faces until it took the photo and Dad was always squinting because he couldn't see the shutter properly."

"Have we still got the seagull photo?"

"That picture is so funny. It totally took out Dad's tripod and nearly ruined the camera. All you see is us in the background at a forty-five degree angle, and half a seagull in mid flight. Dad was not happy."

"We should get that photo framed and put it up."

They were interrupted as Carol's phone alerted her to a message.

"Oh somebody loves you," said Janice.

"Probably the bank again, saying I've got a statement or something. Oh nope, it's Aunty Laura. *'Jack has had the snip, he's not happy. Lol'*. With a smiley face."

"Do you think she knows Lol is laughing out loud? I'm pretty sure she thinks it means lots of love."

"Well she has come a long way, she used to start her texts with, 'Dear whoever', and finish with 'Yours Sincerely', like a formal letter. I sat with her once as she asked Google a question and when Google came back with an answer she typed in *'Thank you'*. I had to explain there was nobody on the other end answering her question, that was a long afternoon. So I can forgive her misusing acronyms."

"Is Jack her new flame? I thought Aunty Laura was in her sixties. I thought she wouldn't have to worry about that sort of thing? Poor Jack, no wonder he's not happy if that's what has happened."

"No," said Carol, "Jack is not her new flame. It's her new Jack Russell. She didn't try too hard to name him. I knew she was taking him to the vet, so this is her updating me. Hang on, she's sent a picture, see," she said, showing Janice a picture of a sad looking dog.

"Awww. That is one sad looking pup. And I would be too if my freedoms of propagating had been taken away. He's probably lamenting all that could have been, if this nasty old hag, who pretended to befriend him, hadn't assaulted him and taken his bits away."

"He's probably entitled to legal representation, but he has no way of flagging up the flagrant violation of his knackers. And the fact that she's broadcasting his humiliation to the world with a *lol* and a smiley face, only rubs more salt into the wound as it were," observed Carol.

"I still don't get that Lol business," said Janice. "I mean, be honest, when was the last time you laughed out loud or cried laughing, like that emoji everyone uses. I know I hardly do."

"Yeah the best I do is smile or grin or maybe a mild 'ha', but just one. Which is quite low level, but never escalates to a laugh out loud or rolling around with laughter," agreed Carol.

"I saw our old dog fart in her sleep once and she woke up startled wondering what had just happened. Now that made me laugh out loud."

"I remember that, she jumped up and looked at where her bum had been. I must admit, I've been there a few times."

The youngsters had quietened down a bit and had found some seats. A few of them were showing each other their socials. Some sweets were being handed around.

Susan had taken herself for a walk up the

platform, as Geoff wasn't really talking and she was getting fed up of trying to put on a brave face, indulging him in his mind numbing hobby. She was close to tears, she wondered where all the excitement had gone, if it was ever there. She was trying so hard to get all the details correct and even uploading their days out on YouTube and social media.

Geoff had topped up his coffee as he reviewed his footage again. He was always worried about getting good footage, because if he didn't catch all the details of the train he would never hear the end of it. Susan was always feeding him details he didn't need to know about and she is always eager to stick whatever she can on that flipping YouTube channel. He didn't even like trainspotting all that much anymore, but she was always organising stuff.

A woman with two dogs came onto the platform. They looked extremely well groomed.

"Oh wow, I love them. What are they called again?" asked Janice excitedly.

"Pomeranians. A toy dog breed from Poland. You can have that little detail for free."

"Thank you. Look at their little legs."

"When I see little dogs like that, I always imagine they are owned by that girl in 'Legally Blonde'." said Carol.

"I know what you mean, but she doesn't fit that description," said Janice, nodding at the owner.

"Not exactly. But there is a whiff of designer about her, her outfit is definitely well thought through. And I certainly couldn't wear a white trouser and look that good. Number one, I don't have tapered legs like hers and secondly anything I eat always finds its way onto my clothing somewhere."

"That's true. I do wonder how you miss your mouth sometimes. I think she looks great, I bet you her house is immaculate and streamline, no clutter. I imagine a white open plan living space, spotless," said Janice.

"Well you would have to be, to keep those trousers clean. I see women driving those small Fiat 500s in pastel colours and cream interiors, I'd have chocolate all over those seats in seconds if I bought one. But she's probably got one of those two seater Mercedes, still with a white interior," said Carol.

One of the Pomeranians was stood on its hind legs, with the front two on the woman's legs as if begging for food. The woman was talking to it like she was talking to a baby. She then pulled out a couple of treats from her jacket pocket. She made both dogs sit before giving them each a treat.

"I'm just jealous, she looks like she is one of those sickening people who look good and are genuinely very nice with it," said Janice.

"How awful."

Janice started laughing. The woman was scrolling through her phone and hadn't noticed anything else that was going on.

"Oh, get a room," said Carol.

"That is hilarious," Janice was properly laughing. "How long do you think before she notices?"

Not long was the answer. While she was distracted the male dog had taken the opportunity to mount the other and was going for gold, when suddenly the two were pulled apart "Hey, stop it you two!" The male dog looked suitably miffed.

The woman looked up the platform towards

Janice and Carol. She saw Janice laughing and grinned herself, she then shouted up to them, "He's at it all the time, I can't get him to stop. At home it's bad enough, but it gets really embarrassing when in public. I've had him done and everything, but he's still like the *Duracell Bunny'*."

"I'd have to be plugged into the mains electric to have that much energy," shouted Janice back to her.

"I ran out of that much energy ages ago." As she said this, she looked back at the dogs, "For goodness sake Boris, leave her alone."

2.19pm

Just then the train arrived.

"All the best with those two. Keep going Boris." shouted Janice as they got on the train.

The youngsters were still laughing and joking as they piled onto the carriage. And Susan and Geoff were back taking notes and checking footage in silence.

All day, trains had been coming and going on the other platform heading west. But no passengers had got off. Not that it mattered to Carol or Janice, although it did make the day more interesting, as many were coming back from work or shopping.

Both had gone silent for five minutes. In that amount of time, a person day-dreaming, like normal dreaming when asleep, can cover a lot of ground and lose track of the world around them. Carol had gone back in time again thinking of her parents. Janice on the other hand had gone in a completely different direction, as was Janice's way. It had always been difficult for anyone to guess what she was thinking, even if they thought they knew, the journey her thoughts took from brain to mouth would prove otherwise.

"Would you have Botox?" asked Janice.

"Say what?"

"Would you have Botox? You know, face and body enhancements."

"Plastic surgery? What are you saying?"

"No, not plastic surgery. Although you could do with it, as you're getting on a bit. I mean injections to get rid of wrinkles, to make people look younger, less tired and so on."

"What's brought this on?" asked Carol. As random as Janice's questions are, they would have had their roots somewhere. A superstar, an advert or a conversation with a friend.

"Well, I saw Adele the other day and she recommended having it done."

Carol was none the wiser. "Is this Adele the pop singer or another Adele?"

"When would I be speaking with Adele the singer? Like that would happen. Do you think I would have been able to keep that to myself for any length of time?"

"That's true. You'd explode if you tried to keep that in. So who are you on about then?"

"Adele down the nail shop. Barbie Adele. She says she gets it done regularly in a place in Taibach. She said it would do me a world of good. I could start with my forehead and go from there..."

"Woah, woah, stop," said Carol interrupting Janice in full flow. "You are seriously taking advice from Barbie Adele? Pouty thick lipped Adele? I've never seen her face move. If you are willing to give up the gift of facial expression, then go for it. And next question. What do you mean 'regularly'? How often does she get it done?"

"Well It's not a permanent thing, it lasts around three months and then you can get it done three months after that."

"You mean, your face is deflating from the moment you get it done? And how much does it cost to inflate your face again?"

"Anywhere between £100 - £350 each treatment. It takes about ten minutes and you're done," said Janice.

"You are done! That's ridiculous, that's £700 a year. I'll poke you with an electric cattle prod for free, and you'll get the same look. But you'll have to buy the prod."

"That is a lot of money! Anyway, I said I don't need it, you can't improve on what I have."

"You are right, there is no physical way of improving that face. Not without a bolster and a lump hammer," said Carol.

"How rude! I did look on the website for other treatments, but I decided they weren't for me either. Everything seems to involve a chemical of some sort."

"I bet the lorry that drops off the chemicals

at the back door has a toxic and flammable safety sign on it. Did Adele also recommend going the whole hog with a complete body wax and a spray tan?"

"Oh, I wouldn't bother with all that, even if she had suggested it. Most of my body doesn't see daylight for the majority of the year, if at all. So that would be a waste of money. Anyway, you still haven't answered my question. Would you have Botox?" asked Janice, again.

"Yes!"

"But you just said how ridiculous the cost was, as well as the lack of movement in the face."

"Well I'm not saying I would go for the full trout pout look. But let's say money was no ob-ject, given in reality I couldn't afford to keep up the constant treatments. Then maybe I would soften some of the lines, to make me look a bit younger. And I am not saying I would consider it now, but maybe in about ten years or so," said Carol.

"Fair enough."

Suddenly, in the distance Pam appeared on

the platform and tried to get their attention. Janice spotted her. "Ay up, Pam is waving at us."

Pam gave the universal sign for '*do you want a coffee?*', raising her hand as if drinking an imaginary cup and raising her eyebrows as if asking a question. The message was warmly received.

Janice gave a big grin and a double thumbs up, the universal gestures for '*yes please*'.

Pam gave a thumbs up in return, which in context meant she had received the positive reply and that two coffees will be coming shortly.

Janice mouthed back '*thanks, love you, you're the best*'.

"Pam is lovely isn't she?" said Janice.

"Yes she's a good girl."

"Hello girls," came a friendly voice from behind.

"Hello Susan," said Janice, "this is my sister Carol."

"Hi Carol." Susan looked a little coy. "Can I chat with you for a minute girls? Geoff is deep into his footage. When he's in the zone he doesn't talk."

"Of course, sit with us for a bit," said Janice.

"What's on your mind Susan?" asked Carol.

"Am I that obvious?"

"Well I don't know about being too obvious, but your mouth is saying one thing but your voice sounds like it needs to let something out," Carol said with a friendly smile.

"Well Janice here seemed so friendly, so I guessed you would be nice too. And well, It's that I just wanted to ask your advice on something. I don't really know why I think you could help or even want to help me, as we don't know each other. But I just needed to talk to someone."

"You get whatever it is off your chest and we'll go from there, you might feel better just chatting," said Carol encouragingly.

"Well it's this trainspotting business. Umm, well, it's, well. I can't stand it. No! I mean I absolutely hate it! It's mind numbing. I do it for Geoff, I get the numbers, locations. I even set up a YouTube channel so we could do it together. But he doesn't talk that much anymore and I'm hating every minute of this mind numbing hobby. I know some absolutely love it, but it's not for me. I want to be anywhere else but here, no offence, but Port Talbot Parkway isn't where I envisaged us spending our time. I want to go abroad somewhere and drink cocktails in the sun, miles away from any trains, tracks, stations. I mean, what do I do? He loves it all, but I'm being driven crazy. I can feel my soul being sucked out of me. I will drop down dead one of these days, and the cause of death on the death certificate will read 'died of boredom'. Not 'died skydiving' or 'jet skiing', but pure boredom."

"That's funny we were talking about how we would want to die earlier," piped up Janice inappropriately. "We didn't even mention skydiving."

"Not now Janice," said Carol.

"Oh sorry, go on. Sorry Susan."

"That's fine, that's it really. I've never admitted all I just said to anyone, let alone to unsuspecting strangers."

"It's something you just have to do sometimes. You should let Geoff know," said Carol.

"Oh I couldn't, it would destroy him. Trains are his world, he was totally into them before he met me, so I wouldn't want to take that away from him."

"I didn't say you should take that away from him. I said you should tell him what you just told us. You need to let him know how you feel, for your own sake and for his. You might be surprised, and it will save him the expense of burying someone who died of absolute boredom. And when he meets his new partner, and she asks him what did your last wife die of, he won't have the guilt or embarrassment of telling her he killed you with boredom. So for that reason alone you should talk to him."

"She's usually right," added Janice. "It's annoying, but it's the truth."

"Maybe you're right, maybe," Susan said looking thoughtfully at the platform floor.

In the meantime Geoff had left his footage, been to the loo and was returning to their equipment. He looked across to three women. Susan seemed to be having a great time with her new friends. What on earth was he doing spending a perfectly sunny afternoon on a train station? What he would give to be strutting down a beach somewhere in his Speedos.

Susan got up from her seat and hugged both women. Her face had changed from an uptight trainspotting face, to one full of relief. She felt the most normal she had felt in a long time. She let go of the two women and walked back to Geoff, who was fiddling with the tripod.

Carol and Janice watched her return, not too long. But just long enough to see Susan take Geoff's hand and get his attention away from the tripod.

Pam came walking out with two mugs.

"Hey Pam, you are a star," said Janice. "How are you getting on?"

"Bill is doing my nut in. He's playing with his new phone, he's trying to choose a ring-tone, going through them one by one, and then trying to narrow it down by repeating the ones he likes. It's like some sort of mental torture, and I'm too hot and sweaty today for that sort of nonsense. If he starts on his message alerts when I'm in there, I'll throttle him."

"If you did kill him, I'm sure the judge would understand, he would probably view it as workplace abuse and downgrade the offence from murder to manslaughter with a suspended sentence. I saw this woman on TV get away with murder because of what she had put up with at work," said Janice.

"I blame the phone companies," said Carol. "After all, we have had mobile phones for decades now, and their ringtones are all flipping naff."

"True," responded Pam. "I'll hold off for now, It's just today, usually he's a good laugh. That and he maintains the coffee machine, so that is a redeeming factor to consider. Anything interesting going on out here, anymore pigeon action?"

"No, no more pigeon action. But the trainspotting couple behind are either going to divorce or will end up stronger than ever," said Carol.

"How do you know that?"

"Oh it's a long story. The short of it is, she hates trainspotting and has never told him."

"Ah, that'll explain the intense conversation going on. I won't look to see what is happening. She does need to tell him though, I saw a couple have a real barney here on the platform, a couple of years ago. They both had 'I love trainspotting' t-shirts on, the notepads, the flasks, even a pair of binoculars. They had been on the platform for three hours before all hell broke loose. She started crying and shouting how she hated trainspotting, I think she had just bottled everything up and then exploded and he ended up demanding she reimburse him for her season ticket that he had bought her, as a one year anniversary gift. They were from Oxford, so that would have been an awkward journey home."

"Ouch, better out than in, as I always say. And not just for unhappy trainspotting girlfriends and wives."

The intense conversation across the platform had stopped and was followed by some packing up. But neither partner seemed unhappy about doing so. They both walked over to three women.

"I've just come over to give you a big hug and a thankyou, to you both," said Susan, addressing Carol and Janice.

"Me too," said Geoff, enjoying the opportunity to get a word in, albeit short.

"We didn't do much," replied Carol.

"You did more than you know, it turns out we both hate trainspotting and we were both afraid to hurt the other. So we're off to book a holiday in Tenerife and drink cocktails by the sea. Hopefully we can get something booked leaving tomorrow."

"Wow, that's fast work," said Janice, "sounds like a great plan, book yourselves a couple of those sun loungers. And do some jet skiing and stuff."

"Well, let's just get there for now, hey? And I'm not sure jet skiing and cocktails mix well."

"Nonsense, I highly recommend it," said Janice laughing.

"Well anyway, you probably both saved our marriage and we are both very grateful," said Susan.

Everyone gave each other a hug, even Pam got a cuddle, even though she hadn't been involved. And Susan and Geoff made their way off the platform. Laughing and joking as they went.

"How do you feel about Botox Pam?" asked Janice, as if the last few minutes hadn't happened.

Carol just rolled her eyes.

"I hope you are not suggesting I need it, said Pam, smiling. "If I wanted a swollen face, all I would need to do is plant my face in a pack of peanuts, and I'd get the same effect. Why do you ask?"

"We were chatting about it earlier, that was all."

"Although, even though I'm not up for it, my Nan had it done once," said Pam.

"What?!" said Carol, who perked up and cocked her head like an excited dog.

Pam started laughing. "Yeah, we were round her house one time and she declared she had been reading some tacky mag, and if it was good enough for Dolly Parton then it was good enough for her."

"She didn't have her boobs done as well did she?" interrupted Janice.

"She would have done, I expect. But once the Botox didn't work out she decided not to try anything like that again."

"Why what happened?" asked Carol.

"Well none of us could see why she should have it done, 'cause even if her face looked better afterwards, it would still look like it was stuck on the neck of a giant tortoise, you know, all that flab. Well anyway, she got herself booked in. They explained the procedure and asked all the usual medical questions as a precaution, they also explained the side effects.

However, what they didn't take into consideration was this was a very elderly lady they were dealing with, and no doubt they had worked on a variety of clients, their usual clientele were not over seventy-five and some questions they didn't think to ask. And most had their own teeth.

So my Nan had it done and was very happy. But it takes two or three days after the injections to see any difference. So on the third day she got up as usual, went to the bathroom, had a wash, got herself dressed, all good. Then she went downstairs to make a cuppa."

"Right? Oh no, go on," Janice was totally into the story.

"Well before she goes to bed at night, she takes her teeth out and pops them in a glass of water next to the kitchen sink. Goodness knows why the kitchen sink and not the bathroom. So she comes downstairs, goes straight to put the kettle on, pulls out a cup and tea-bag. While the kettle is boiling she uses the waiting time to stick her teeth in. Only that she found she couldn't get them in her mouth. What had happened was, she had a whole load of botox injected around her mouth, she looked like Donald Duck once it took effect. And her mouth wouldn't open as it did before and she just couldn't fit her teeth in."

Carol and Janice started laughing with Janice getting doubled up.

"I tell you something, she wasn't laughing, well she couldn't for one. When we came round after a frantic phone call, we all just stood around laughing, it took us ages to compose ourselves and to be of any use. Anyway, she did find a way of getting them in."

"What was she like eating and drinking?" asked Carol.

"Yes, well, that was another thing. It took her ages before she could drink a cup of tea without dribbling everywhere or using a straw. Soup was a definite no go. For anything else she had to develop a technique so that she knew when she had the complete fork full in her mouth. It was ridiculous, honestly," said Pam.

"I bet. No wonder she didn't have plastic surgery on her boobs too. She'd poke someone's eye out, and getting her shoes on would have been a struggle," said Janice.

"We've never let her forget it."

"That is so funny," said Carol. "It's like she had an extremely late midlife crisis, a latelife crisis. Brave woman for having a go though."

"She's a woman and a half. We've had a scream over the years."

"Like what else?" Janice was thirsting for more now.

"Did I never tell you about when she had the grandchildren and the new puppy round?"

"No!" said Janice. "What happened?"

"One Saturday morning we had to go into town for some bits, nothing major, but to take the kids would have made everything twice as long. So we left them with my Nan. However, you've seen Arthur recently, haven't you? Our Staffie. He's a lot bigger now. Well, he was only a pup at the time and we left him there with her as well as the kids. So off we go to the shops, and we come back an hour and half later. We walk through the front door and there's absolute chaos. My Nan is scrubbing the floor, the pup is stuck in a shoe, and the kids are just crying in the living room. They looked traumatised, so she knew something bad had happened."

"Oh my life, and your kids are usually really good. What was wrong?" asked Janice.

"So when we left, Nan had the TV on, the kids were playing with the pup, all very nice. And you remember I said my Nan left her teeth downstairs. Well, she was always leaving things she shouldn't, just lying around. To give a bit of a back story, Nan had trouble eating chips, pasta, anything heavy, all that kind of stuff bunged her up. She'd been to the doctors and been recommended some tablets to get everything moving."

"Oh no," said Carol. Who could see where this was going. Janice hadn't clicked yet.

"The kids had gone from the front room to playing upstairs and the puppy had also gone with them. Unfortunately the kids came across the tablets the doctor had given her and thought they had found a pack of sweets, they thought they had hit the jackpot and helped themselves and then gave a couple to the puppy. They all came downstairs and little Gemma had offered them to Nan. Nan's eyes must have been like saucers when she realised what had happened and she also knew time was ticking.

Anyway, by the time we came through the door, the puppy had emptied itself in the hallway, in the dining room, in the kitchen. And so had the kids, only they had tried to make it to the toilet upstairs. They had all failed, and a wet brown streak was left on the stairs."

"Oooh. you mean they were...?" the penny dropped! Janice was now up to speed.

"Laxatives. Yes. The poor kids didn't know what had hit them or what they had eaten, they just sat there in the living room crying, like I said, traumatised. Nan had taken their clothes off them and chucked them in the wash, and washed and wrapped the kids in towels. We were there for hours cleaning up, even then we had to get a professional carpet cleaner in. Nan couldn't really shout at the kids because she realised it was ultimately her fault. So that was another story we remind her of every now and again.

"I'd say that was cruel, but I can see how that would be too funny to let go," said Carol.

2.15pm

The trains had become a bit more frequently since 2pm. Trains coming from Cardiff had mainly been passing through, even though they did stop, nobody had really got off. And now it was coming up to mid afternoon, fewer passengers were getting on the trains heading the other way.

"Could a member of staff please report to the security office," came a male voice over the platform speakers. It was more of an instruction than a request.

Pam rolled her eyes. Her moment of peace and quiet had been interrupted. "I will kill him you know, one of these days."

"Is that for you then Pam?" asked Janice.

"That's Bill's way of saying it's time for the fish and chip run. I did say I would get some for him. Obviously he can't shout that over the tannoy."

"He must have finished with his phone. So every cloud and all that," said Carol.

"Well that's positive, I guess. Would you girls like anything while I pop over to the chip shop? My treat."

"O what do you think Carol? We were going to get some pies on the way back home. But if you're buying, I won't say no to a small chips and a minced beef pie please." Janice wasn't one to turn down food.

"I have eaten, but I can't resist pie and chips either," said Carol. "Yes please, pie and chips, if that's ok with you?"

"Of course, and it'll give me an excuse to pop down to you guys again. Once Bill has been fed, I won't hear from him again usually."

2.30pm

The train from Swansea hadn't long left the station, and it wouldn't be that long before it reached Port Talbot Parkway.

"I think we're going to need to start again, and make a new batch."

"Jenny hadn't seen anything on her boat and unless you remember where you left the box, we will need to start over, that's going to be fun inviting everyone back."

"It was a nice day out regardless, remembering all the things I'd forgotten."

"I just hope we don't get caught. It was a close run thing last time, you know how people talk."

"Do you think anyone would know what to do with the box if they found it?"

"I doubt it. It's probably landfill by now," said Eunice.

"That's not very eco. I need the loo again," said Jack.

2.42pm

The next train from Swansea pulled into the station as Pam walked off to get chips.

"Right, I need the loo," announced Carol.

"You've done quite well today, you have usually gone a few times by now."

"I think it's the heat. Being in the cold makes

me want to go more often. So with this heat I don't need to go that often."

"The fascinating inner workings of Carol's bladder, tune in next week for bladder watch." announced Janice in her best mock voice over voice.

Carol headed for the toilets.

The 2.42pm train had departed. An elderly couple came past Janice.

"Jack! You've only just been," said the elderly woman.

"I know, but I will need to go again before we head home."

"I hope you haven't flushed your bus pass away, I'm not applying for another one."

"Untwist your knickers dear, I've got it here in my pocket."

Janice was laughing to herself, it was hardly a private conversation, being so loud.

"Hello," said Janice, raising her voice. "Had a day out then?"

"Oh yes. We've been to Swansea for the day," said the elderly lady.

"Oh, she's nagged me to death. I need a lie down," said the elderly man.

"Oh shut your face."

"We went for a walk down the Mumbles, she couldn't keep her hands off me, *'Jack give us a kiss'*, every two minutes. She can't resist me when I'm wearing my teeth," said Jack laughing to himself and giving Janice a cheeky wink.

"He's always like this. He would have left the house without his teeth if I hadn't reminded him. He nearly left the house the other day without putting his trousers on, he had just his long johns on."

"You say I forgot. You just didn't want me giving the other ladies in the street a thrill."

"Or a heartattack."

"Did you go there for anything special?" asked Janice.

"It's our Anniversary. Forty-four years this year. So we popped to some of our old haunts down the Mumbles."

"We just go for an ice-cream, sometimes a meal," said Jack. "I can't do the Mumbles mile anymore, my bladder won't take it. So we keep it simple. And if Eunice is lucky she gets a kiss and a cuddle," said Jack, being careful not to give anything away.

"Are you sure Eunice is the lucky one?" asked Janice laughing.

"Of course she's the lucky one, not everyone gets a kiss and cuddle from a specimen like me."

"Especially with your teeth in and trousers on," affirmed Janice.

"I don't know how I resist sometimes. If you told me forty-four years ago, I'd still be getting a kiss and cuddle from the same bloke, I wouldn't have believed it. And now he's bald, blind, deaf, has false teeth and walks with a limp, what could be more attractive," said Eunice.

"And I had a wash this morning and put clean underwear on especially for today. That's why she's so excited, I usually do that once a week."

"Wow, now that is special! You are right, your wife is a lucky woman, not every husband would be that thoughtful. And she gets to see you with your long johns on, I'd love a man like that."

"Yes, and if I'm really lucky I get to wait outside the men's toilets every two seconds, as he needs to go all the time."

"I told you already, when they replaced my hip, they whipped my bladder out at the same time and put in one belonging to a mouse. Speaking of which, I need to go."

"I feel like his carer sometimes," said Eunice.

"That's a heavy rucksack you have there, are you ok carrying that?" asked Janice.

"Oh don't worry about me, between my pilates class and swimming each week I can handle this quite easily, it's Worzel Gummidge here who struggles."

"Come on, I'll go for a pee and then we'll get you back in your coffin before dark," said Jack, again giving Janice a cheeky wink.

"I'll bury him in the garden one of these days. I'll take him away, have a nice day love," said Eunice to Janice.

Jack and Eunice headed for the loo, just as Carol was coming back.

"Bye both, don't kill each other on the way home."

"Have you made new friends again?" asked Carol.

"Yes, a lovely couple, funny and adorable.

He's a mischievous old man and she could kill him. How's your bladder now?"

"All good, I'm set for another session."

"I was flicking through my phone earlier and you know there's a Port Talbot Historical Society?" asked Janice.

"Yes, Dad for all his tech phobias, couldn't resist joining the Facebook page."

"Yes well, I was hunting through the web page and I never thought I'd be a part of history so soon, after I'm dead yes, but not now," said Janice.

"What on earth are you on about now? I'm sure you are sniffing something every time I go to the loo," said Carol.

"No, seriously," said Janice, "remember Princess Anne came to open the Civic years ago?"

"Yeah, what about it?"

"Well I found a video in the video section of the website. I can't remember if you were still in school or just about to leave that year. The school let us out to see the opening, and I remember clear as day, standing on Station Road, behind the barrier waiting for Princess Anne's car to turn up. Somebody had recorded it, and

I'm on that video somewhere in the crowd and now it's on a website dedicated to Port Talbot's History," said Janice, "but the issue I have is, I'm not old enough to be considered a historical figure yet, I'm the present, surely?" asked Janice emphatically.

"Janice! That's over thirty years ago. That's history in anyone's book. If you go back thirty years before I was born, World War Two was coming to an end. Sorry to break it to you, thirty years is a looong time, you is old, you is history, living history maybe, but history all the same."

"Okay, don't rub it in too much. As long as some grubby kid doesn't come up to ask me what life was like when I was young. I haven't long left young, it's very fresh in my memory, and I would like my memories to gather some dust before anyone asks me that," said Janice.

"Well yes, I'm with you there. Give me another couple of decades before asking me those sorts of questions. Plus I need enough time to think of something to bore the poor kid to death with, to make sure he or she never asks that ever again, and I want to be able to enjoy the torture."

"Well what's the point in living that long, waiting for those old person moments to arrive and not enjoying them. I want to be able to use expressions like *'Kids today, they don't know they're born'*."

"Or what about any sentence that starts with, *'In my day'* or *'when I was young'*?" suggested Carol.

"Oh those are good. I would also like to have a stick to point and wave at them as I said, *'I would have got a leathering for saying things like that'*, said Janice.

"Oh and *'I blame the parents you know'*."

"Yes definitely! A *'you know'* on the end of any sentence would make anything you say sound old."

"Talking in itself is old fashioned these days. You'd probably have to text a 'you know' as a 'YK' and then use a 'BTW' and a 'LOL' at the end," said Carol.

"You do realise the longer this conversation goes on, the more I'm realising how old we are getting. There ain't no young people having this kind of conversation. We really have crossed the line well into middle-aged going on old."

"Okay it's your turn to stop right there. I can still get away with wearing a pair of leggings like the young people."

"Your head and heart might be telling you that, but your middle-aged butt is telling a whole different story. And it doesn't lie. Gravity has taken hold of your butt and it isn't going to let go. It has gone south for the summer and stayed there. It..."

"Alright, alright," interrupted Carol, "you can, in the words of the Spice Girls 'stop right now'. Your's isn't much better."

"Hey, my head and heart tell me it's tight as a drum. I'm not interested in the truth, I'm happy to live in denial and listen to my head and heart."

2.47pm

The 2.47pm arrived at the platform, trains were now coming relatively thick and fast.

A young man covered in tattoos and a cello disembarked.

"Now that's a lot of tattoos," said Janice.

Carol hadn't been looking who was getting on or off. "Where?" she said looking around. "Oh yes, that is a lot! I'm not sure I could have that many, especially not around the neck."

"I don't think I could sit still long enough to have anything done around my neck, I'd be afraid I'd move suddenly and get stabbed by the needle. That would be a sad way to go."

"Do you think some of these youngsters have thought it through? I mean he's young and everything will stay in place for the time being, but what happens when he gets a double chin and everything else heads south. Surely his tattoos will sag too one day?"

"Oh do you remember Phil Williams from college?"

"Just about," replied Carol.

"You'll remember he was a fit young man at the time, always down the gym. Well we were in the canteen one time and he took his top off to reveal his new chest tattoo. To be fair it had been done very well. It was a woman in the middle of his chest with a pair of eagle wings stretching across his whole chest. Lots of detail and colour. We were all impressed and had the bonus of seeing him with his top off. Anyway I caught up with him a couple of months ago."

"Is he still fit and slim as you remember him?" asked Carol cynically.

"Obviously not. He's almost thirty years older and the years haven't been kind. I saw him and his family as we walked down the promenade, it was very sunny and he had his top on once again. A couple of kids, mortgage and good eating had taken their toll. He had evidently stopped going to the gym and had taken up going to the pub instead. The years hadn't been kind to the tattooed woman either. She was now sitting, perched on his beer belly looking like she had given up on life and her wings had drooped down along with his moobs. The detailing had become blurred and the colours had faded."

"It's really sad when it goes all 'Pete Tong' like that," said Carol.

"It evidently had become a constant reminder of what he had been years ago. Although it may not have actually bothered him as he was happy to have it on show," said Janice.

"Or maybe he still thinks he's seventeen, eighteen. And he means to go back to the gym soon."

"Maybe, but I doubt it. His wife was pretty though."

The young man with the tattoos and a cello was now messing with the cello case. He opened it up and started checking over its contents.

"Do you think he's part of an orchestra?" asked Carol.

"Well he's hardly a one man band. And you don't see too many solo celloists."

"It's cellists. And what I meant was, do you think he's a part of a proper travelling orchestra or plays in a theatre, that kind of thing?"

"I would hope so. It's a lot of effort to learn an instrument like the cello and not be a part of a group or have a place to play it. Unless he goes busking with it."

"Yeah maybe, I have seen buskers playing random instruments in Cardiff. I saw one who played the oboe one time, he wasn't too bad, but he played dreary tunes all the time. I felt depressed listening to that going from shop to shop, I wanted something jolly. Can you play anything jolly on a cello?"

"Jaws," replied Janice almost immediately. "Not a jolly tune maybe, but would certainly make me laugh, and would make me jolly."

"That would be funny. Although you couldn't keep that up too long."

The young tattooed man had closed his cello case and wheeled it towards the lift.

The air was still warm, a little less intense as it had been, it had become now more pleasant and comfortable. And both sisters went quiet again as they enjoyed the moment.

Carol closed her eyes again and became more mindful of the warmth on her skin, the gentle breeze, and traffic as it passed. She thought of nothing else for what seemed like an eternity, but was probably only for a few minutes, five at most.

"Do you remember whatshisface? The chap who used to wear a tartan skirt around town, he tried passing it off as kilt?" And in one swift sentence, Janice revealed that she hadn't been so mindful, blissfully enjoying the heightened sensory experience of a warm zephyr. But as usual, her mind had gone so far away from Carol's it beggared belief.

"Do you mean *'Kilted Ken'*?" asked Carol without questioning how Janice had got on the subject.

"Was that his name? Kilted Ken?"

"I wouldn't have thought so, I think we just used alliteration for effect. I think his real name was Hillary Jones. What about him?"

"Oh nothing, I was just thinking back to school when we walked through town at lunchtimes, he always seemed to turn up by the old library. He always seemed really happy, not in an off his face kinda way. But in a, just had the one can of Cider kinda way."

"He probably had, it was lunchtime after all."

"How did you know his name was Hillary Jones? Did you ever speak to him? I know I didn't. I would have been too scared to talk to him," admitted Janice.

"I don't know, somebody must have said to me one time. Because I never spoke to him either. He liked to have a little jig, I do remember that. He must have had a second Cider for dessert. That or the first had a stronger effect than I thought."

"Funny how we remember random things sometimes isn't it?"

"Yeah. I remembered Port-hole Bill earlier, do you remember him?"

"Oh yes, I remember him!" said Janice as a vision of Port-hole Bill came to her mind. "Now there was a man who was always on the hobble. At least he was happy to do some work for his beer money, bad work, but work all the same."

3.09pm

The 3.09pm arrived at the platform and a number of passengers got off the train. Some carrying evidently new clothes after an afternoon shopping spent in Swansea. A mother and her kids got off and made their way to the exit. And finally a man with a fold up bicycle got off and carried it as he went.

"Would you get a bike again?" asked Janice.

"I doubt it, I haven't the desire or the energy to use one. And where would I go on a bike anyway?"

"Not even an electric bike?"

"Have you seen the price of them? No thanks. I nearly got knocked over the other day with one of those. I would have got really angry, but then I noticed it was blind Alice. How she doesn't have more accidents I don't know."

"Well she was bad enough on a normal bike. Do you remember she ran over her neighbour's cat?"

"Oh yes, that was bad. The screech was horrendous, she was lucky not to have killed it. It walked with a limp until it died years later."

"And its tail had to be removed. She would have definitely killed it on one of those electric bikes. Have you seen how fast they go?"

"Well yes, as I just said she nearly killed me on it. Knowing Alice's luck though she'd avoid killing anyone on the street, but electrify herself plugging it in. Do you remember we took her to A&E after she decided to cut an electric cord with scissors because she thought it was too long, while it was still plugged in?"

"That was a tough one to explain to the doctors at the hospital," said Janice. "I had to repeat myself three times before they understood what had happened, because they couldn't believe someone could be that stupid. I held back from telling them she would have been in A&E sooner if we hadn't stopped her from trying to trim a hedge with a chainsaw."

"Where she got a chainsaw from I don't know, she didn't own one. And it wasn't her hedge, she was only doing old Mrs Evans a favour. It looked a proper mess afterwards, Mrs Evans was not happy and she made sure Alice paid for the damage."

"Maybe we should 'borrow' her bike one time and get someone to lower its maximum speed. Like they did with Aunt Reenie's mobility scooter, after she pinned that poor woman to the shelves of the bread section of Lidl, when she accelerated too quickly."

"I'd forgotten about that," said Carol. "I think Aunt Reenie blamed the scooter, saying it shot forward by itself."

"Didn't she die skydiving? Heart attack or something?"

"Yes, she put on the health and safety forms they asked her to fill in, that she didn't have any heart conditions and that she was fully fit, she even told the instructor she had recently completed a 5k disability charity swim and came second. She didn't tell them she had recently had a triple bypass and technically was still in recovery."

"That poor instructor, I bet he had to have counselling afterwards."

"I think the school tightened up its policies after that. I think you need a reference from your doctor if you are over fifty now, thanks to her."

"Didn't they play *'My heart will go on'* by Celine Dion at her funeral?" asked Janice.

"Yes. I spoke to her daughter after the funeral and she only realised what she had asked for, after the event. Her mother really liked the film Titanic apparently, and it didn't occur to her it might not be the most appropriate song. She said it was a happy mistake, as her mother would have found it hilarious and the family have a happy memory to remember her by."

Just then Pam could be seen coming down the platform with a bag of goodies.

Janice was the first to clock the bringer of gifts.

"Here she comes, Pam you are an angel, a uniformed angel bearing glorious gifts."

"I am and don't you forget it!" said Pam handing warm packets of deliciousness.

"Thanks Pam, what do we owe you?"

"Think of this as a prezzy."

"Are you sure?" asked Carol.

"Well, technically I didn't buy them, Bill paid for them. However, I had the thought, and as everyone knows it's the thought that counts. And he won't care and I won't tell him, not until later at least. He should be stuffing his face as we speak, so let's all look up to the camera and wave."

All three women turned and faced the camera and proceeded to smile and wave.

"I am warning you now," said Pam, turning back to the two women. "Drug-Dealer Dave is on his way over, he's off to Cardiff for the evening."

"Why are you warning us, is he going to offer us his wares?"

"Unlikely," said Pam.

"Does he still think he's a drug dealer?" asked Carol.

"Is Dave not a drug dealer then?" asked Janice, unaware of his true identity.

"No," said Pam, "he watches too much telly and has a vivid imagination. He likes to pass himself off as a dealer and a gang leader. But everyone who knows him, knows he's harmless. He hasn't a clue how to get hold of drugs, he'd have trouble sourcing paracetamol in a pharmacy and he has the menace of a newly born lamb skipping with puppies in a grassy meadow. Albeit a very ugly unwashed lamb in a leather jacket from the nineties."

"So why are you warning us then?" asked Janice.

"Well he seems to have left his dark underworld activities behind him and he now claims to be a Muslim. I just had a whole conversation about his journey to Islam and how he was going to a Mosque in Cardiff to worship."

"What are we going to call him now? Especially now he has left his former lifestyle," asked Carol.

"Ah, yes, well that's another thing. He no longer wants to be called Dave but he's telling everyone to call him Ali Baba."

"Seriously?" asked Carol in disbelief. "Does he have any idea who Ali Baba is?"

"What do you think?" replied Pam, smiling. "Of course he doesn't. And I didn't have the heart to tell him everyone in these parts thinks of Ali Baba as a fictional character. Everyone down the pub is more than happy to call him Ali Baba. I mean who's going to look that comedy gift horse in the mouth?"

"So are you warning us because he might come over and try to convert us?" asked Janice.

"Well not exactly, it's just he may come over and bend your ear about his new life and I'm just giving you the heads up. That was all."

"Oh I see," said Janice, "not to worry, it won't be long before his train arrives, so he can't be here too long."

"These chips are lovely by the way," said Carol, popping a hot, salty, vinegar soaked chip in her mouth.

"Good aren't they? Right! I'm going to leave you two gorgeous female specimens here and head back to the bat cave and see what Hawk-eye is up to."

"Thanks Pam, see you in a bit probably,"

said Janice as Pam headed back to the security room.

"Ali Baba! What a plonker. He really does watch too much telly!" said Carol, her hand slowly popping chips in her mouth and savouring each one.

"Or maybe not enough telly or the right programmes. When…," said Janice interrupting herself mid sentence to allow the next chip to enter her mouth, "was 'Ali Baba and the…," another chip entry, "Forty Thieves' last on the…," incoming chip, "telly?" Her hand, unlike Carol's, was now in perpetual motion from her packet of chips to her mouth, carefully synchronised with her minimal chewing action and swallowing each mouthful.

"Goodness knows. It's probably on some hidden Freeview channel somewhere. Dave only watches Netflix these days. His journey to Islam couldn't have taken that long, he was only telling me the other day he was expecting a shipment of drugs from Columbia last week. He doesn't even know where Columbia is, let alone have contacts there. I bet you what's happened, he's watched some biodoc of Muhammad Ali with one of his mates. His mate has said you should do that, convert to Islam, he's ran with it and his mate probably suggested his new name to boot. Knowing full well Dave is easily influenced and wouldn't have a clue."

"Funny though," said Janice

"True. How's your pie?"

"Lubbly," said Janice, her mouth full of pie.

Meanwhile Pam had made her way from the platform and into the hive of activity that was the station's central nervous system - the security room, headed by one of the sharpest minds of the security world, also known as Bill.

Bill was still making his way through his chips as she came through the door.

"Have you got my change?" asked Bill.

"What change?" asked Pam nonchalantly.

"I gave you £15. You and I didn't eat £15 worth..." a penny was dropping as his sentence slowed down and came to a halt. "Oh I see, very funny, that's why you were all waving at the camera. Very funny."

"It was a heartfelt wave of gratitude Bill, they were touched by your generosity and were very appreciative."

"I bet they were."

"Could you pan the bus stop camera and let me know when you see Drug-Dealer Dave?" said Pam pointing towards the screens.

"Ali Baba? Have you seen him then?" asked Bill.

"Yes, I bumped into him as he came out of the chip shop and he told me about his conversion. Alison from the Police station has asked me to give her a text if he comes onto the platform."

"Why what's happening? They don't think he's a real drug dealer do they? They are not that daft surely, are they?" asked Bill.

"I doubt Alison would have asked me to give her a text unless something was up."

"Okay, but it's only daft Dave. He's harmless," said Bill.

"I'm not too sure about that. I have my suspicions he's not as daft as he makes out," said Pam.

"What do you mean? He's dull as a brush."

"I always thought that, but the other night as I was going home, I saw Dave sat in a BMW with a blonde woman in the driver's seat. Nothing too unusual I know, but there was a look in his eye. A more sinister kind of look, not the look of a daft wannabe. I've never seen him like that before."

"I am sorry to repeat myself, but this is daft Dave we are talking about. He's all mouth and no trousers. Nobody in their right mind would have him under surveillance."

"There," said Pam pointing at a black car parked on the side street, "zoom in on the black BMW."

Bill zoomed in.

"That's her, that's the woman. And look on the bench."

"Which bench?" Bill was now really concentrating.

"That bench, with the couple on it. You know nobody stops there and sits on that bench. I think they are watching the woman in the car. I wonder where Alison is."

"There's your man now, he's just appeared."

They watched daft Dave pass the black car, stop for a brief moment and then cross to walk towards the train station.

"He's coming this way," said Pam. "I'll wait

until he's actually on the platform before I text Alison."

"Did you pick up some curry sauce to go with my chips?" asked Bill, looking around but seeing no evidence of a curry pot.

"Pass me your rubbish and I'll pop it in the bin," offered Janice.

"Lovely thanks."

"I was going to ask," said Janice. "Where do you fancy going on holiday this year? Have you given it any thought?"

"Not really, have you?"

"I'd like to volunteer looking after bears in Transylvania."

"Not a caravan in West Wales then?"

"No! But honestly it's a real thing, that or killing Lionfish in Belize, but I would prefer Romania as it's closer."

"Naturally. Where do you find these things? As much as I'd like to babysit a Romanian bear in the woods or whatever it is, I'd much rather prefer to go to a quiet little town somewhere or seafront here or some sunny island and drink coffee or a glass of wine, followed by walking some back streets looking for things of interest."

"How about Sardinia then?"

"That's more like it."

"Oh good, they have Europe's largest sink-hole we can visit and some awesome grottos."

"Do they have beaches?"

"Yes."

"Wine?"

"Yes."

"Somewhere to drink it?"

"Yes."

"Then I'll be doing that while you go looking at a hole."

~~~

"Have you told Carol and Janice anything about this? Are they in on it?" asked Bill.

"I've only just let you in on it. And besides I was told to tell no-one, and you're no-one so I can tell you. But it goes no further, do you understand?"

"Who am I going to tell in here? There's only you and Phil that come in here, and Phil
~~~

has kept himself to himself today and the odd guest. What is going to happen? Is it some sort of sting operation?"

"I have absolutely no idea. All I was told was to keep an eye on him. Alison wouldn't say any more than that. So something or nothing might happen. I wouldn't get your hopes up though."

~~~

"Do you know who I haven't seen today?" asked Carol.

"Do you want to narrow it down or just tell me?"

"Uniform. Craig, Alan, Sheryl, nobody in a high vis, nobody with a PC badge. Do you not find that strange?"

"No. It's a sunny warm day, they are probably plodding down the promenade with an ice-cream or in the town centre. Nobody came round last Saturday so I wouldn't expect anyone today."

"That's true. Oh look, here he comes, Ali Baba."
~~~

"He's tall," said Janice, never afraid to state the obvious.

"Is it true Dave? You've changed your name to Ali Baba?"

"Alright Carol." Dave turned to Janice, "Hello."

"Hello there," responded Janice.

"I've been on a journey Car, I've been en-lightened, and yes I've changed my name to Ali Baba."

"Can I call you Al then?"

"I suppose. I haven't been told I can't shorten my name."

"Have you read the Quran then?"

"Not yet. I've downloaded it to my phone. I'm off to Cardiff to meet a fellow worshipper I met on Facebook and learn more. I might stop for a drink first in 'Spoons when I get there, no point rushing."

"Yes you want to pace yourself, it's a long journey you're on. You know you can't drink alcohol now right? What's brought all this on?"

"I wanted to better my life and I found what I was looking for."

"Nothing to do with the new Turkish family

that moved into your street and their extremely beautiful two daughters then?"

"Well, umm, well, no! I have been around their house, and I have spoken to the Dad, but only for enlightenment. Hence my trip today."

"Enlightenment? Is that what you are calling it these days, is it? Drug-Dealer Dave wasn't cutting it, was it? Did they know your former life?"

"I didn't feel it was the right time to mention it, I thought I'd wait a little bit first."

"Hey!" Piped up Janice. "Do you know you will have to wear a tunic now you're a Muslim? So that swanky leather jacket will need a new home. Do you want to give it to me now or after you've got your tunic?" Janice knew this wasn't true, but she thought she'd try it on. Just to see if she could his jacket.

~~~

"We're on!" said Pam. There was a sense of excitement in Pam's voice. "I'm texting Alison." She put her glasses on and typed as quickly as
~~~

she could. Old school typing, two thumbs on either side of the phone.

"You text like an old woman. You'd swear you've got an old Nokia 6310 not a smart phone. You know you can swipe these days."

"Not now Bill. I'm concentrating."

"I can see that, your tongue is sticking out. What are you typing, is it an essay?"

"No, I've put *'visual on target, he's on platform'*," Pam said, acting like she's on some crime tv show.

"What's that Guv? you got a visual? Do you wanna take him down Guv?" mocked Bill.

"Shut up! How often do things get this exciting? And besides I'd make a great D.I."

Pam's phone bleeped. "It's Alison, she says, *'Thanks, great stuff'*."

Pam and Bill stared at the monitor as Dave chatted with Carol and Janice.

"Here comes his train," said Bill, tapping on a different monitor with his finger.

~~~

"You're train is here Al," pointed out Janice.
~~~

"Oh great," said Dave AKA Ali Baba.

"All the best on your journey Al. Let us know how you get on. Remember, no alcohol! Not even a shandy."

"Oh thanks very much. Yes, I'll keep you informed."

Dave's train arrived, he thanked them again and boarded the train. Nothing happened.

~~~

"Was that it?" asked Bill.

"I told you not to get excited," said Pam.

"Don't pretend you didn't want to see some sort of action. You were all, 'visual on platform guv', earlier."

"Okay, I was hoping for a bit more, and Alison hasn't said anything further."

"What you need now is a strong velvety coffee."

"That sounds really nice, thanks Bill."

"Well if you are making one for yourself, can I get a cappuccino?" said Bill with a tongue in cheek smile, leaning back on his chair, hands behind his head.
~~~

Pam looked at Bill in disbelief, shook her head, smiled, and then turned to the coffee machine and made them both a cuppa.

Bill then leaned forward and stared closely at one of the monitors.

"You know that black BMW you had me zoom in on earlier?"

"Yes, what about it?" Pam asked, without turning around.

"Well there seems to be some activity around it."

Pam stopped what she was doing almost immediately.

"Where?"

"Here, look." Bill tapped the monitor.

The BMW was surrounded by plain clothes officers and some uniform. The blonde woman was now out of the car. She had been handcuffed and was being led to an unmarked police car.

"Well, there's your action," said Bill.

"Well who would have thunk it? No wonder Alison was very brief. She was still monitoring the BMW."

"That coffee ready?" asked Bill.

~~~

Across from the station some commotion was happening.

"Hey Carol, there's some sort of bust happening over there," said Janice, perking up.

"It's probably nothing. Somebody has probably gone into the back of another vehicle."

"I don't think so, I would have thought we would have heard a crash if that's what it was. There's a lot of people for a crash, I can't really see what's going on."

"You know what it is like around here, if nothing is happening, nobody is bothered, but as soon as there's the slightest action everyone wants to get involved," said Carol cynically.

"Who is this Turkish family then, they've moved into Oakwood Street?"

"Yes, not far from us, about fifteen doors up from Dave 'Ali Baba'. They are lovely."

"How do you know that?" asked Janice.

"I spoke with them. I popped in as I was passing the other week. They invited me in for some food and a drink, so I wasn't going to turn
~~~

that down and they were great fun. I will tell you one thing for free, they aren't daft."

"What do you mean?"

"Well I wasn't there too long before they told me about our friend Al. And guess what they referred to him as, Drug-Dealer Dave. They were totally clued up, there are no flies on them. They've not been in the area long, but they've wasted no time getting settled in and trying to fit into the community."

As they were talking a smartly dressed, slender woman came down the platform. She looked professional but friendly.

~~~

"How on earth did she get on the platform?" asked Pam, still in the security room. "Goodness me, she's stealthy."

"That's our Alison, I heard she used to be *Special Forces*, not that you can tell just from her looks. I learnt that from Terry down the pub, he's usually right about stuff like that," said Bill.
~~~

"Well if Terry said it, then it must be true. I wonder what she wants with the girls?"

"Well I'd imagine, since he was chatting with them, she'd want to tap them for more information," said Bill confidently.

"Yes ok, but I thought she was concentrating on the woman in the BMW?"

"But she also asked you for a text. And she does have access to our CCTV."

"Does she?" said Pam, the inflection in her voice rising as she said it. "I didn't know that."

"Well D.I. Perkins, that's why you are platform staff and I'm used for security. But I'm no-one, so what would I know?"

"Hurt did it? When I said you were no-one."

"Did a bit," said Bill.

"You'll get over it, don't choke on your cappuccino."

~~~

"Hello girls! How are you getting on?"

"Oh hello," said Carol. "Haven't seen you in a while, where have you been?"
~~~

"Since I've been back, there's been a lot to be getting on with," said Alison.

"I like your outfit," said Janice. "Very smart, it screams, *'I mean business'*. A long way from your Tesco outfit, I missed my checkout buddy after you left."

"Sorry Jay, you were the best checkout buddy I ever had, if that's any consolation?" said Alison.

"Why on earth would you leave scanning endless groceries to join Special Forces and travel the world? You could have been a supervisor if you'd played your cards right."

"That was the dream, but it wasn't to be, what can I say?"

"Hey Alison," interrupted Carol, "I was saying to Janice earlier I haven't seen any uniform on the platform today. Usually somebody pops over to say hello, not even Sheryl has come over."

"Sheryl is on light duties, she's patrolling the seafront."

"So what brings you over here Al? Has it anything to do with the bust over the road?" asked Janice.

"Sort of. You were chatting to daft Drug-Dealer Dave earlier. What did you chat about?"

"Is this official duty?"

"It is I'm afraid! I can't tell you anything just now, wait until we go out for a bottle of wine and I can fill you in. So what did he say?" asked Alison.

"Nothing much really, nothing I didn't already know. He's pretending to be a Muslim to impress the new Turkish girls in his street, and he's off to some mosque in Cardiff, he didn't say where," said Carol.

"He did say he was going to 'Spoons first though," said Janice.

"Oh, did he now? That might be useful. And that was it?"

"Pretty much," said Carol. "He wasn't here long before his train came."

"Thanks girls, you've been very helpful. And look I was serious about that drink, are you available over the weekend? We should be done by then and it would be nice for a good old catch up."

"We're always available, especially for a glass of wine or two."

"Hey, perhaps we can push the boat out and have a meal," said Janice.

"Steady on Jay, I'm not as flush as you," said Alison with a warm smile. "Look I've got to go, but I'll be in touch. Kisses to you both."

"Thanks sweetie, speak soon," said Janice, as Alison made her way to the security room.

3.48pm

Dave's train had left almost ten minutes ago.

Alison reached the security room door, she pushed down on the handle and crept into the room. Bill and Pam were fixated on the monitors.

"Hello, hello, hello," said Alison.

Both Bill and Pam jumped out of their skin.

"What the...oh my life, you made me jump, how did you sneak in here?" asked Pam, re-covering.

"Alright Al? Pam is making a cuppa if you want one," said Bill with a rye smile.

"Are you Pam? That would be lovely. Ta, you're a gem." Alison was fully aware Bill was pushing his luck.

"So what's going on?" asked Pam, loading the coffee machine. "All these mysterious texts, saying something of nothing. Drug-Dealer Dave surveillance and arresting strange women."

"Can't say," replied Alison.

"What do you mean you can't say? Me and Bill are fully invested in this secret operation of yours and you can't say? I'm gonna need more than that if you want to get out of here alive."

"I mean, I genuinely can't say. I'm under oath. It's an ongoing operation. But don't worry I'll treat you once we're done, promise. You know, if I could tell you, I would!"

"I know, I know. So how are you going to treat us then?" asked Pam, handing Alison a mug.

"How does a night out sound? You, me, Carol and Janice? A couple of bottles of wine and a meal, in that order."

"Oh sounds good, just let me know when. I could do with getting my glad rags on. Will there be a bit of karaoke?"

"Don't push it Pam! I'll drink with you, but I won't sing with you, I draw the line there on our friendship."

"Hey, what do I get?" asked Bill.

"A kiss and a cuddle," said Alison, giving Bill a thumbs up.

"How about an Indian take-away and a lager of my choice instead?" replied Bill.

"How rude!" said Alison, feigning an offended look. "Of course, I'll put it on expenses."

"In which case, I'll be ordering the works."

"Quite right! Just order whenever you want and send me the receipt and I'll get it paid courtesy of the local constabulary. I also came in to thank you both, you've been more help than you realise. And I'll spill the beans as soon as it is over. Anyway I have to go before they send a search party, thanks for that," said Alison handing back the empty mug, "I needed that, and remember I love you both."

~~~

"It was lovely seeing Alison today, even if she was on duty. It's been a while," said Janice.

"It's nice when you have friends and when you see them again you can pick up where you left off."

"We got into so much trouble working
~~~

together, and yet they still kept us next to one another on the checkout. She seems to be doing well."

4.00pm

The station clock turned to 4.00pm. It actually read a satisfying 16.00.00.

"What's that noise?"

"What noise?" asked Janice.

Carol looked up the track. "There she comes, get your camera out." A black shape was coming down the track, not quickly but steady and it got larger and clearer as it chuffed closer, smoke billowing from its smokestack.

"Goodness me, I'd forgotten all about that." Janice fumbled for her phone, turning on her camera.

"I wonder what train it is?"

"It's a pair of Black Five engines 45407 and 44871."

Carol turned to look at Janice. "How on earth do you know that?"

"Geoff and Susan told me. Remember that trainspotting couple?" The locomotive loomed large as it entered the station. It had no intention of stopping. And Janice captured it as it came past, with all its carriages behind. She panned her phone as it went past and headed off into the distance. It even gave a blast of its whistle. "Well you don't see that every day!"

"It came so suddenly, unexpectedly. I'm still taking it all in. They are such beautiful engines," said Carol, staring down the track still fixated on the locomotive puffing away.

"I'm just glad I got it on camera, that's one for YouTube," said Janice, reviewing her footage. "And just think Geoff and Susan missed out on it."

"How did you remember the engine numbers?" asked Carol.

"I don't know, I just did. I didn't really think about it, stuff like that gets lodged in my brain and comes out when needed, and when it isn't. It's as bizarre to me as it is to you. It did come and go quickly though"

4.02pm

The 4.02pm to Swansea pulled up at the

station. It seemed a quiet arrival compared to the noisy locomotive that had passed through.

Janice recognised the regulars getting off, some of which she saw getting on in the morning.

Carol and Janice allowed things to remain quiet for a moment. The stillness of the platform punctuated the more busier times. And was something to be savoured.

Janice was the first to break the silence as usual. Carol would have been happier for the silence to have been longer, but neither did she mind the distraction.

"I saw Wally on Station Road a couple of days ago."

"How was he? He's obviously out of prison."

"Yeah he's fine. He had just been to the Job Centre and was popping into the charity shops, he said he was looking for a jacket or something, as you do," said Janice.

"How long was his sentence?"

"I think he was sentenced to three years but was out a year early on good behaviour, he's still on parole for the time being."

"Knowing Wally, he's after a Jacket for a

specific job. He never stops, he's always going from one scheme to the next. That's how he ended up inside, for doing some elaborate job he was working."

"Real estate, wasn't it?" asked Janice.

"Did I not tell you the full story?"

"No, what was it?"

"Well you know Lucy Mills? He was seeing her before he got put away. Well the reason they are no longer together is because he nearly got her arrested too."

"No way? She's really sweet, she would have been eaten alive."

"Yeah, the only reason she didn't get arrested is because she had done everything legit on her end, paperwork, registered with the taxman, etcetera. What she didn't know was, that he was only posing as an estate agent, she thought that's what he actually did, he passed himself off as freelance, so never questioned why he didn't have a proper office."

"So what was he doing exactly?"

"He was advertising land on Facebook in the local area. That was his first mistake. The land was real, it just wasn't his to sell or have permission to sell. He was selling parcels of land to small developers, faking the paperwork, fake bank accounts and hoping he wouldn't get caught. One plot of land had four houses on it before anyone questioned what was going on. I think the land belonged to a farmer, and because the land was in a seldom checked area of his property, it went unnoticed for months. By which time Wally had walked away with half a million."

"So how did he get caught?" asked Janice.

"Yes, well this was where Wally's genius came to an abrupt end. The farmer and developer had come to an arrangement which benefited them both. The developer would obtain the proper planning permission for the site, finish off the houses, and take a generous cut of any profit made off two of the houses and the farmer would lease the land, own two of the properties outright to sell or to rent. And both would work to make sure Wally was caught."

"So how did they get him?"

"So they first of all got the police involved. Then all parties agreed on an operation to draw Wally out from wherever he was hiding, which wasn't far it turns out. The developer would totally flatter Wally and say how happy he was with the property and offered even more money for another plot. And Wally couldn't resist. Wally arranged to meet at another made up plot down Margam way, the developer turned up with the farmer as his so-called business partner and the rest you know."

"That's bonkers. I wonder what he's got in the pipeline now?"

"Best not to know," said Carol. "Whatever it'll be, it will involve stitching somebody up and something very illegal."

Pam appeared on the platform and went to see Phil, who was pottering around.

Janice's phone bleeped.

"Angela has just sent me a text," said Janice.

"What about? What is she up to now?"

"Okay, she says, *'Hi babes x, looking to start a women's Sandfields rugby team, all are welcome, looking for volunteer players and coaches, regular venue. Any suggestions welcome. Had a great response so far. Do you fancy it? Kisses to Carol xxcc.'*"

"I thought she was running a football team? What happened to that?" asked Carol.

"Half the team got pregnant. She only had thirteen girls and six of them were out of action three months in. And Sharon poached the rest for a team she had set up weeks before."

"So where is she going to get fifteen girls for a rugby team plus a few more for subs?"

"I did already know she was organising this. She was handing out fliers to all the girls at the Diet club, which was subtle," said Janice. "Hold on, she's sent an image." Janice flicked through her phone in search for the photo, "Goodness me, she's fully kitted out in a rugby kit. See!" Janice showed Carol her screen.

"Oh wow, she's gone for it. She's like a female Adam Jones, that shirt is a size too small, surely?"

"Yeah, I'm sure the tape around the head is unnecessary. What does she have in her mouth?" Janice tapped on the photo and used her fingers to zoom in on Angela's mouth. "Oh my life, it's a gum shield. I think it has 'av a go' written on it."

"Ask her what she means when she says, she has had a good response."

"Okay give me a second."

In the meantime Carol received a text off Alison.

'Have you seen an elderly couple today? Alison.'

'No. We saw a trainspotting couple. Carol.'"

'Okay, thanks xx.'

"Angela says, she's got a few from the Diet club, Suzi and Les are also on board, and a couple from the boxing club. So seven players. Aberavon RFC have been kind enough to let them use some of their training facilities and has put her in touch with a former coach who is at a loose end. So it sounds promising for her by the looks of things."

"Aw that's good. Hopefully she can get it off the ground. I'm sure the twins will be able to recruit a few," said Carol.

"The twins are absolute monsters, Suzi put a bloke in intensive care once after he tried to nick her handbag. How he couldn't tell she was a weightlifter I'll never know," said Janice.

"Didn't Les and Suzi come one and two in the Welsh championships?"

"They did, Les has slowed down a bit since then, and Suzi has entered fewer competitions this year, so they are probably looking for another avenue to channel their energies," said Janice.

"I wouldn't want to be on the receiving end of a tackle from those girls." Carol then remembered the text she had received, "Alison also gave me a text asking if we'd seen an elderly couple today, which I thought was a bit random."

"Well we have, Jack and Eunice, you'd popped to the loo and they left as you were coming back. What did you tell her?"

"Well I said no we hadn't. I'll text her back now, she didn't say why she needed to know if we'd seen an elderly couple. I doubt she will tell us anymore information once I give her an update." Carol then proceeded to send a message back to Alison, who got back almost immediately. 'What time?' Alison is asking what time you saw them.

"They got off the 2.42pm train from Swansea, I'm sure of it."

Carol waited for a reply from Alison after sending her the time. *'Great thanks'* was the reply.

"Is that it? Isn't she going to give us any more than that?" asked Janice who was expecting much more.

"You know Alison isn't going to say more than she has to. She is good at what she does."

~~~

Bill was sitting quietly in the security room. Occasionally looking up to see if anything was happening on the monitors. Nothing. The most exciting thing to happen had passed. He carried on doing a crossword he'd started lunchtime.

All of a sudden an extremely loud notification came from his phone and he nearly fell off his chair again.

"Goodness me that was loud," said Bill, quickly turning the volume down. "That needs adjusting. What does Alison want now? She can't be wanting an invoice this soon."
~~~

Bill adjusted his glasses, "Let's see, *'Hi Bill, can you send me a copy of the CCTV footage from 1.30-3.30pm please? I'll explain later. Thanks hun'.* Why does she need that? Nothing happened." He texted back, *'No problem, I'll give you a text once I've emailed them to you'.*

4.07pm

"Do you think our pigeons will return before we leave?" asked Janice.

"Maybe, if they live here, they may want to hang around the station before settling down for the night."

"Do you think they have a bedtime routine?"

"I doubt they make themselves a hot chocolate or have a glass of wine watching the sun go down."

"Well it would be nice if they did, I could go home happier knowing they were settled and comfortable more than I would have done not knowing," said Janice.

"You don't think that elderly couple has anything to do with Drug-Dealer Dave do you?"

"What do you mean? They got on and off

different trains, at completely different times to each other," said Janice.

"Well don't you think it strange we don't see or hear from Alison for a long time, which isn't unusual in itself, but then all of a sudden, not only do we get interrogated about Drug-Dealer Dave, we also get text messages asking about the whereabouts of a seemingly unrelated elderly couple on the same afternoon. Just a bit strange that's all," said Carol.

"I suppose, they could be witnesses to something I guess. I really hope my pigeons come back soon."

"Maybe, I could be overthinking things."

"Wouldn't be for the first time," added Janice. "Do you remember you anonymously reported Mrs Davies to social services because you were worried she had dementia and knew her family didn't visit? On the basis she kept going back and fore to her shed for no apparent reason."

"Well it really seemed odd and out of character. How was I know she was breeding puppies in there? I thought her bitch Luna had died ages ago."

"You didn't think to ask her if she needed

help, how her dog was or if anything was wrong like a normal person? Not you, you go straight to the authorities to report her and diagnose her with dementia. I know I can be daft at times, and I really admire your intelligence and usual careful forethought. But sometimes, just sometimes, you seem to lose it, you seem to have some sort of brain fart and do something really stupid."

"I'm just glad they don't happen that often. Just because when they do happen they are more embarrassing than anything else," said Carol.

"Although I must admit, you did extremely well to keep a straight face when Mrs Davies came round to tell you what had happened when social services came round and how she spent a couple of hours doing dementia quizzes before they were convinced she was as sane as the rest of us."

"Well thank you, not my finest moment, but thank you," Carol said gratefully.

"On a different subject, I think I'm going to compose my email to the RSPB on the routine of the pigeons based at Port Talbot Parkway."

served them to the family. But just as they were about to tuck in, his mother double checked one of the mushrooms in her book and immediately ordered everyone to stop. Because apparently even though this particular mushroom was edible as soon as you had alcohol with it, it releases all it's toxins and that's the end of you," replied Pam.

"Carol releases toxins too as soon as she has alcohol."

"Funny!" responded Carol. "Very true though."

"That would be a rough way to die. Imagine wiping your whole family out, including yourself. You might not be found for days or months," said Janice. "How do you spell pigeon?"

"Hey? Why do you want to spell pigeon?" asked Pam, confused.

"I'm writing my report for the RSPB and we've established the PT Parkway pigeons have a lunchtime routine, so I'm letting them know and I'm hoping they come back to the station to roost. It is birds that roost, isn't it?"

"P, I, G, E, O, N, pigeon," said Pam helpfully. "And yes birds roost."

"Great, thanks," said Janice, typing pigeon on her phone.

"What did Alison want earlier?" asked Pam. "She seemed to appear from nowhere."

"She is stealthy that one. She just asked about Drug-Dealer Dave or Ali Baba as he says he is now apparently. She didn't say why she wanted to know. I guess she came to see you guys in the office afterwards. Did she say anything to you?" asked Carol.

"Not really. We could see a woman being arrested across the road, but she didn't comment on that either. There were no juicy titbits thrown our way," replied Pam.

"I know there's something going on, but I can't work out what. No uniforms visiting the platform, Alison popping up on duty, that woman getting arrested and text messages asking about elderly couples. All on the same day. Nothing that exciting happens around here. And the most suspicious thing of all is that Alison isn't letting on about any of it."

"Right," said Janice. "I've got, *'Hi, my name*

is Janice, I thought you might like to know my observations regarding the pigeons that live at Port Talbot Parkway station. I believe they have a lunchtime routine, as they stay on the platform all morning and then leave in the direction of the town centre. I noted the time as around 11.45am. I thought you might like to add this information to your database. If you need any further details please feel free to contact me any time on this email. Feel free to forward this correspondence to Countryfile or Nature Watch, Kind Regards, Janice.' What do you think?"

"It's lovely Sweetie," said Pam like a patient parent pacifying her child while the adults are talking.

"And Bill doesn't have any other info?" asked Carol.

"Not a dickybird. I'm sure he would have said more if he had anything. You know what he's like, he can't keep anything secret," said Pam. "What elderly couple? She didn't ask us about an elderly couple.

"Bill would probably explode if he had to keep anything in, and she only contacted us some minutes back about the couple," added Carol.

"Okay I've sent that to RSPB headquarters, I am sure that valuable bit of information will be added to their vast database," said Janice.

"There'll be an excited OAP on the other end dressed in a RSPB anorak forwarding that intel straight to the pigeon division, those in duck and other wild fowl divisions will be so jealous."

A text message pinged on both Pam's and Carol's phones.

"It's Alison," said Pam.

"I got one from her too," said Carol.

"*'Forget Ali Baba, false alarm, working off bad intel. See you on the weekend. xx.'* That's all she's put," said Pam reading out the message.

"Same here. That's disappointing, I was hoping for something more juicy. Janice was hoping for some drugs bust earlier," replied Carol.

Another ping, but this time only Pam's phone. "Another text from Alison, *'Have any unusual packages been found at the station over the past few months?'*"

"This is getting frustrating, there's something going on, it has to be under our noses and we can't see it."

"Any unusual packages?" said Pam thinking out loud.

"How about that black and white telly?" said Janice helpfully.

"How's that suspicious?" asked Pam.

"Well who leaves a telly behind? Did you check it for drugs? Counterfeit money? Text Alison, perhaps CID will be straight over to fingerprint it." Janice was getting into this now, especially now her brain had been cleared of pigeons. At least for the moment.

"It was just a TV Janice. And it wasn't left on the station, it had been left on a train and it needed to be offloaded somewhere and registered, so it was deposited here for processing."

"How about those false teeth? They were left here," asked Janice.

"How are they suspicious? There were definitely no drugs or money hidden with them," said Pam.

"Yes, but it wasn't just one set of teeth was it? It was fifty sets in their boxes. Did you check all the boxes? Or check who left them or when?" persisted Janice.

"I suppose. But I can't imagine Alison being interested in a box of false teeth. I will have to check the lost property later and I'll ask Bill if he's seen anything. I'll give Alison a text later," said Pam.

4.30pm

"Woah." Janice's eyes lit up in amazement.

Both Carol and Pam immediately shot a look down the platform to see what Janice was gawping at.

"Don't make it obvious you're staring," said Janice.

"Janice! Your mouth is gawping like a gold-fish, maybe rearrange your face to something more subtle first," replied Carol.

A fine looking young black man had come onto the platform. He must have been at least six foot seven, and that was without the Afro. He had a Jimmy Hendrix style headband as if in his honour. What really completed the look was the psychedelic flares he was sporting.

"Now that's a look," said Pam.

"What year is it again? Have I gone back in time? He looks so cool," Janice was transfixed.

"You should get yourself a selfie Janice," said Pam smiling, knowing once the idea was planted in Janice's brain, it wouldn't take long to germinate before she would go for it.

"Oh my life, yes! Where's my phone?" Janice quickly fumbled for her phone.

"He's coming this way," said Carol. "He looks confused."

The young man was now walking straight towards the women.

"I bet he's from the RSPB, he's seen your report Janice," said Carol dryly. Pam smirked.

"Oh I do hope so," replied Janice.

He approached the three women and addressed Pam.

"Excuse me, do you work here?"

"I do," said Pam.

Janice's neck was bent backwards trying to get a good look at the young man.

"I need to get on the train to Bristol, which side of the platform do I need to be please?"

He asked politely, in a strong Bristolian accent, which took the women by surprise.

"I love your accent, where is it from?" asked Janice, unable to contain herself.

The young man looked down at Janice and smiled. "My accent is from Bristol."

"Is that where you're from then?" said Janice, she had automatically blanked out Pam and Carol.

"Yes, me and my accent. Do you know it well?"

"I went to Ashton Gate once to watch the football, do you like football?" Janice was on a roll, questions were just falling out of her mouth without thinking.

"Ummm." came an awkward reply.

Carol decided to rescue the young man. "It's this side," she said, pointing at platform two. "Excuse my sister, she doesn't usually get to speak to men."

"Can I have a selfie?" blurted Janice.

The young man looked at Pam and then at Carol, as if they were her handlers and both gave a gentle nod indicating he'll be fine and it was safe to proceed. "Yeah, okay, that'll be lush," he said.

Janice leapt to her feet, phone in hand. Simultaneously turning her back towards him and facing the camera. The young man put his arm around Janice and had to crouch so both of them could be seen in the image. Both gave a smile at the camera and Janice took the picture.

"Oh thank you very much, that was great," said Janice.

"No problem."

"The next train will be here in five minutes love," said Pam, after Janice had had her moment.

"Thank you, that's kind of you. Have a lovely day." He said as he moved to a more socially acceptable and safer distance down the platform.

"Well he was a nice young man," said Janice.

"To be fair you wasted no time there Janice. You scared the life out of him in the process mind you. But credit where credit is due," said Pam.

~~~
~~~

Bill was half watching the security cameras and half on his phone playing a game. His phone bleeped. Now was this an email or a text message. He had set the alert tones differently for both emails and messages. It was a text message.

"It's Alison, what does she want? Have I seen any suspicious packages left on the platform or anywhere at the station? No!" He typed back immediately. "Oh I'd better get a copy of those recordings to her nibs as soon as," Bill said to himself. He had gotten used to talking to himself. He set to work getting a copy emailed over to Alison.

4.42pm

The 4.42pm train pulled up to the platform and the young man waved a second thank you to the three women and boarded the train.

"He was 'lush', and really tall," said Janice.

"There you go," said Carol. "And you got a selfie to remember him by."

"I'm going to pop back to the office to quiz

Bill, to see if he is aware of any suspicious packages. That, and I need another coffee."

"It's those boxes of false teeth, I'm telling you. That's not something you just leave behind at a station. Or you need to open up that telly. And I'll have a cappuccino please," added Janice.

"I'll come with you to the office, for the same reasons as you Pam," said Carol. "Are you okay by yourself for a bit?" she asked, addressing Janice.

"I'm sure I'll manage without you guys for a bit," replied Janice.

Carol and Pam left Janice where she was.

Janice leaned back and again enjoyed the alone time and warm breeze. No one else was on the platform, except Phil who was pottering at the far end.

She allowed herself a small yawn. She closed her eyes, that felt nice, she was semi-conscious when her head started to nod. She listened to the traffic which became like white noise in the background. She nodded a couple of more times. The warm air seemed to wrap around her like a warm blanket. Finally her head gave up the fight, falling gently onto her chest, her jaw also fell open. It wouldn't be long before she would be dribbling. Bill kept an eye on her just in case anyone decided to take advantage of the situation.

~~~

Pam opened the door to the security office, come tearoom.

"There he is, Port Talbot's answer to *Batman*, in his bat cave ever alert to fight off the criminal fraternity. Or at least ready to call the police. No point in risking life and limb, is there Bill?" said Pam.

"Too right! What's up *Robin*, my faithful sidekick?" replied Bill. "I see you've brought *Catwoman*."

"I'll take that as a compliment, thank you Bill. At least I'm not *Alfred*," said Carol.

"What coffee do you want?" asked Pam, presenting the coffee machine like an old fashioned gameshow model displaying the big prize.

"An Americano please. Thank you," replied Carol.
~~~

"Do you want one too Bill? Don't want you getting drowsy on duty."

"No thanks, I've not long had one and my bladder isn't what it was. I'm keeping an eye on Janice, she seems to have dropped off."

"That didn't take long," said Carol. "She'll sleep anywhere that girl. Anyway, what's news Bill?"

"Nothing, all quiet here." Bill pushed his phone to one side.

"Rubbish! Alison has been in touch hasn't she? What has she said? I know when you are lying Bill, don't make us do good cop bad cop on you." Carol really did know when Bill was lying, she had never failed to call his bluff.

"Okay, but don't tell Alison. She did text me. She wanted to know if I had seen any suspicious packages on the platform. I told her, no I hadn't."

"And what else?" asked Pam without turning around as she made the coffees.

"Nothing!" said Bill like a guilty suspect in a murder inquiry.

"Bill!" Even Pam knew when he wasn't telling the whole truth.

"Am I that obvious? I was practising my sincere face all afternoon, because I knew you two would interrogate me."

"It's hardly interrogation Bill, just some simple inquiries to help with our investigation," answered Carol.

"Investigation! What investigation? Who do you think you guys are? I think the heat has got to you two today. A couple of text messages and a little bit of excitement and you guys go off on one."

"A couple of messages? So there were more than one then?" Carol was definitely 'bad cop'.

"Ummm..." Bill really was useless.

"Bill, you may as well tell us. Carol has got her game-face on, you've had it now." Pam was definitely 'good cop', the oil between the cogs. She handed Carol her americano.

"Alison asked for CCTV footage from 1.30-3pm. I've just sent it to her. What on earth is going on?"

"We don't know," said Carol. "But something's up. Alison is asking questions of all of us. That woman got arrested earlier. And why would she ask about a suspicious package if she didn't think there would be one?"

"There's a whole load of junk in the lost and found cupboard if you want to have a look. But it's just the usual stuff, umbrellas, hats and some odd bits. Anything of value left on the station or a train is sure to get nicked straight away," offered Bill.

"Come on, I'll show you where it is," said Pam. "I'll bring madam's cappuccino."

~~~

Janice became aware she had been sleeping. She was aware her eyes were shut as the light tried to penetrate her eyelids. She was cosy warm. She just had to remember where she was. Her consciousness hadn't fully engaged with the outer world yet. 'What day was it?' 'What am I doing today?' Her brain was reluctant to help. Okay something was coming back to her. She blearily opened one eye. She was definitely outside. The image started to become clear as she opened the other. Then everything came flooding back.
~~~

She pushed herself up in her seat, as it hadn't taken her long to slump into position as she slept. "Goodness me, how long was I out for?" she said out loud, "that felt like hours." She looked up at the clock and tried to work it out. "Fifteen minutes. I was well gone. Where is everyone?"

~~~

Meanwhile in the middle of town. An old woman was sitting on a bench next to the river near the 'Mortal Coil' statue. Not that any of her pigeon company would care. She had bought herself a bag of chips with a small sausage. She had them smothered in salt and vinegar and savoured every one. She finished the bag and chucked the crumbs on the floor. A familiar pigeon and his lady friend wasted no time to rush to the fallen bounty. The old woman put her rubbish in the bin and then pulled out a bag of toffees. It had been years since she could enjoy a pack of toffees, since they ruined her old false teeth. Her new pair were a dream, she had been assured they were toffee proof and had no
~~~

need to worry. She was sure to test that promise out, as this was her third bag in a week. As she chewed on them she watched the pigeons hoover up the crumbs. They didn't last long.

~~~

Pam pulled out her keys to the lost and found cupboard. It was cleaned out every couple of years. And by the looks of things a couple of years had already come and gone.

"If you need an umbrella you know where to come," said Pam, switching on the light.

"You're not short of kids clothes either are you? Let me know when you are clearing out and I'll pop them straight onto Ebay. That'll pay for a girls night out."

"Do you need one of these?" asked Pam, holding up a prosthetic leg.

"Seriously, you'd think someone would know if their leg was missing. What do you think we are looking for? What does a suspicious package look like?" asked Carol with her head in a box of clothes.

"I don't know, I doubt it's drugs or weapons
~~~

as Alison would have employed some sniffer dogs to give everything a once over. So I doubt she even knows what she is looking for."

"Do you reckon we should pull this TV apart?" asked Carol, twisting a small black and white television set so she could get a look at the back.

"Does it look tampered with? I am sure that came off a train some time ago, but not recently. We could check the pockets of all the clothes but that would take ages and they have never struck me as suspicious," said Pam.

"There's nothing in these suitcases, they are all empty, which is odd in itself." Carol pushed the last suitcase back into place.

"You'll be surprised, normally it's students or holiday makers who forgot they had an extra case for duty free," replied Pam.

"Here is the box of false teeth. Each box has Dutch writing on them. Who buys a job lot of teeth from Holland? They can't all be for one person, surely?" said Carol, opening each small box.

"That's true, they don't look cheap either. I thought false teeth or dentures were made for individuals, don't they take a mould first? Do they have individual markings on them?" asked Pam.

"Yes they do. The inside of the lid has a name followed by a number. Each one is different. I still don't understand how that could work or why you'd buy a boxful."

"Maybe they're an order," suggested Pam.

"Maybe," said Carol. "that's the only thing we've found that is strange, I'm not sure about suspicious though. Do you want to be the one to text Alison and tell her we've unearthed some suspicious dentures?"

"When you put it like that. Shall we go and see if madam has awoken from her slumber. Her cappuccino will be getting cold.

5.00pm

While Carol and Pam had been playing detectives, Janice had remained where she was.

"Well?" asked Janice as the two women returned. Carol handed Janice her drink.

"Well what?" asked Pam

"Well what did you find out? My cappuccino

has cooled down quite a bit, so you guys must have been up to something. So what did you find out? Did you find any packages anywhere?"

Carol and Pam filled Janice in with all they had got from Bill and hunting the lost and found cupboard.

"So it is the false teeth," said Janice excitedly. "I knew it. Have you told Alison?"

"Have we told Alison we have found a box of false teeth and we think they are suspicious for no reason? Ummm no," replied Carol.

"You should, it could be important intel that," insisted Janice.

"Did you enjoy your sleep?" asked Pam.

"How'd you know I fell asleep?"

Pam pointed at the camera. "Bill had his eagle eye on you, just in case somebody came and tried to rob you."

"Aw that was nice of him. I did actually. I had no idea where I was when I woke up or what day it was. It was bliss," replied Janice.

"Look! I've got to check on Phil to see if he needs help with anymore cleaning. Keep me posted," said Pam, "If you don't see me, I'll probably be in HQ with Bill." She made her way back up the platform to find Phil, who had decided to make his own tea and was sitting happily sipping away with a biscuit, something he had mastered over the thirty years he had been working on the platform.

"Okay, will do," said Carol.

"So you are not going to text Alison then?" asked Janice, addressing Carol.

"No. There's nothing to report. How could dentures have anything to do with that woman getting arrested or the CCTV footage. Any sign of your pigeons returning?"

"Not yet. But I was asleep for a quarter of an hour, so anything could have happened in that time."

There hadn't been any passengers waiting for some time. Then suddenly an older gentleman came on to the platform.

"Is that who I think it is? It can't be. He wouldn't be by himself, surely?" It was Carol's turn to stare at other people on the platform.

Janice turned to look to see who Carol was staring at. "Get off, that's not him."

"It certainly looks like him. He hasn't got his stick though."

Both women were now staring trying to work out what was wrong with what they were seeing.

"Tom Jones is shorter than him," said Janice eventually, "he has to be a looky likey. That can't be our Tom for real."

Carol sent Pam a text. *'Who is the Tom Jones looky likey?'* She could see Pam in the distance check her phone.

She typed quickly on her phone and looked back to Carol, *'Frank Richards, he's probably got a gig tonight. Don't know where.'* It was a silent conversation only interrupted by a message notification indicating it was the recipient's turn to respond.

'Is he any good', Carol didn't bother with too much punctuation.

'Yeah very good, even clears his throat like him too'.

'Does he have his money' replied Carol, adding a smiley face.

'I doubt it, Frank shops at B&M, I reckon Sir Tom is a Waitrose guy.'

'You know he's from Pontypridd? He's not that posh.'

'Okay, Asda's George.'

'*More like it.*' Carol gave a nod and stuck a thumbs up to Pam and that indicated the end of that conversation.

Carol turned back to Janice, "He's called Frank Richards, he's a Tom Jones impersonator."

"Ah, that makes more sense." Janice turned and shouted down to Frank, "O Tom, sing us a tune." Carol bowed and shook her head in embarrassment.

Frank however enjoyed the attention and needed very little prompting to entertain. He almost immediately slipped into total Tom mode. One hand held an imaginary microphone and the other did all the Tom gestures,

"*What's new pussycat? Whoa, whoa, whoa,*

What's new pussycat? Whoa, whoa, whoa, whoa,

Pussycat, pussycat, I've got flowers and

lots of hours to spend with you,

So go and powder your cute little pussycat nose,

Pussycat, pussycat, I love you, yes, I do,

You and your pussycat nose."

Frank sang the whole opening verse walking towards Carol and Janice.

Janice was totally loving it, even Carol had to smile. Bill could see something going on from his office but couldn't work out what was going on.

"Wow, well done Tom, that was great." Janice stood up to applaud.

Frank stopped and gave a bow. Lapping up the applause. "Available for bookings anytime," said Frank with a wide smile. He handed Janice a business card.

"Ooh lovely, thanks Tom. Or is it 'Frank the Voice - Tom Jones tribute act'?"

"Frank will do. Are you a fan? Of Tom I mean not me," said Frank, smiling.

"Big fan. Well, I'm from Wales, I have to be. I think that was the first law passed by the Welsh government at the Senedd, so no choice really," said Janice.

"I didn't know that, but it makes total sense. And we are all probably related to him too."

"I'm sure of it. My father met Tom's cousin's gardener once, so that makes us kind of related I guess."

"Without a doubt. Well in that case, the honour is mine," said Frank gently bowing.

Carol decided to join the conversation. "Do you have a gig tonight Frank?"

"I do, a couple getting married have booked me for their wedding in Swindon. I perform tomorrow evening, but I need to run through a few things with the happy couple tonight. I like to meet in person, you never know, I don't like nasty surprises."

"Very wise. How do you get bookings? Facebook or do you have a website?" asked Carol, interested in the admin as usual.

"All of the above, and I also have an agency who books me for various events."

The 5.13pm approached the station.

"Here's me now," added Frank as the train pulled in. "Hopefully we'll see each other again."

"Thanks for the song Tom," said Janice. "O quick selfie Tom." Janice whipped out her phone in a flash. They both posed for the photo as the train came to a standstill. "Thanks Tom."

"No problem, any time pussycat," said Frank getting on the train.

"Love youuu Tom!" shouted Janice as Frank disappeared into the carriage.

"Goodness knows what you would have done if that actually was Tom Jones," said Carol.

"I'd think I'd pass out with excitement," said Janice as they watched the train pull away. "Him and Kelly Jones of the 'Phonics'"

"Naturally."

Both went quiet for a short while. Each in their own world, as was their custom.

5.18pm

Carol eventually broke the silence, "I'm going to write a list."

"What kind of list?" asked Janice.

"Of events. All this business with arrests, odd text messages from Alison about suspicious packages and whatnot."

"You want to save your brain power for 'Pop-Master' and crosswords. You'll burst a blood vessel trying to link things together," Janice said looking at her phone.

"I'm going to do it. Where's my notes app?" Carol pulled out her phone.

"Hannah from the mobility shop has sent me a text. She's asking, would you be willing to get involved in a race she's organising?"

"Why didn't she text me herself? Why is she texting you?"

"Does she have your number?" asked Janice.

"Oh I don't know, probably not."

"So it's not just me then that has brain farts. If she hasn't got your number she can't text you, can she?"

"Does she know I can't run? Or fast walk for that matter?" said Carol.

"You won't need to. It's not that kind of race."

"I'm not riding a bike neither. I got chafing the last time I rode a bike. So that's not happening."

"No, none of that. She is organising a mobility scooter race around the centre of town. Starting this end of Station Road towards the Aberavon shopping centre. Turning left at Tesco before the bridge and through the B&M entrance. The course winds through the shopping centre and back out again around the fountain and a sprint back down Station Road."

"But I don't have or use a scooter. And she's got a cheek if she thinks I'm old enough to need one. So where do I come in?"

"I'll ask." Janice texted Hannah back. "How's your list coming on?"

"I'm ignoring your false teeth theory for a start. I have got down all I mentioned earlier and I reckon we need to see that CCTV footage to see any suspicious passengers getting on or off the trains." Carol mused as she went over her list again.

"What does a suspicious passenger look like? Are we looking for someone in a trench-coat wearing dark glasses smoking a cigarette?" asked Janice, "Hannah says, being old isn't a prerequisite for entering the race. She just needs twelve racers, she has ten just now and needs two more. Also her insurance has stipulated that contestants musn't be high risk, for example prone to high blood pressure."

"That'll rule out all those in care homes."

"History of angina or heart attacks."

"That rules out half of Port Talbot."

"Clinically obese."

"No wonder she's struggling for contestants."

"Can you with all good conscience say you aren't clinically obese?" asked Janice.

"Half of me isn't, the other half of me, I'm pretty sure I could get in race trim for the event. When is it?"

"Saturday."

"What? This Saturday? That might be a push. Tell her yes, I'm sure I can make time, I'm up for it. Do I need to get a crash helmet, ask her?"

Janice obediently texted back.

"I reckon my pigeons will come home to roost soon," said Janice.

"What makes you think they live here?"

"I don't know for certain, but If I was a pigeon I'd live here. Free from predators, mostly quiet at night, dry and there's a digital clock so I know what time breakfast is. Ideal I'd say."

"Who am I to doubt your pigeon knowledge? Well, let's see what happens."

"Hannah says don't worry about crash helmets. They are providing bicycle helmets for all contestants with the race sponsor on them along with gloves and knee pads."

"How fast are these mobility scooters that I risk wrecking my knees?" asked Carol.

"You were asking about crash helmets earlier. How many OAPs do you see wearing crash helmets?"

"How many do you see wearing knee pads?"

"Do you know how to drive, is drive or ride correct? Anyway, do you know how to use a mobility scooter?" asked Janice.

"Nope, but I'm sure I'll pick it up. I just hope I get a fast one."

~~~

Meanwhile, not too far away at the back of a small terraced house, in a converted shed.

"Ok Enid, stay still and try not to talk, pass me the alginate. I'm so sorry we are having to do this again."

The alginate for the denture mould was dutifully passed.

"Okay Enid, bite down.....That's good, it should only take a minute......And open wide......Excellent! Well done Enid. Just a moment. There you go all done, rinse your mouth out, we'll make sure it's a rush order. And remember, mum's the word."
~~~

"Thank you," said Enid

"No problem, I'll text you when they are ready for collection. Say hi to Bert from me and tell him I'll pop round for my onions tomorrow and tell him I've a set of broad beans he can have."

5.25pm

"What do you mean I come out with stupid stuff?" asked Janice, "it's true."

"I'm not disputing whether it's true or not, but who is sending you this stuff?"

"Well I think it's mind-blowing and funny all at the same time, and it's Weightwatcher Jenny if you must know sending me all this stuff. It's true though 'Your fingers have fingertips but your toes don't have toetips yet you can tiptoe but not tipfinger'. Poof," said Janice, making the appropriate sound effect to match her hands doing the universal 'mind-blowing' gesture.

"Talk about mind-blowing, look who's just returned from our glorious capitol," said Carol nodding in the direction of the latest arrival.

"How did it go Dave?" asked Janice loudly.

"He was a no show," said Dave.

"Oh I'm sorry Dave, do you want to talk about it, what happened?" asked Carol, trying a bit of sincerity to see if it suited her or not. She wasn't sure whether she pulled it off or not.

"Well, I got off at Cardiff Central Station and headed to Riverside. I arrived a little early at the Mosque and waited outside for a while. And no one came. After an hour, one fella turned up to worship, I told him why I was there and he said it was a scam, I was the fifth this week. Different people had been turning up all week expecting the same thing as me, only to be stood up and waiting outside the mosque for ages."

"So what happened after that bombshell?" Carol decided sincerity didn't suit her, but she was happy to fake it for a bit.

"Well I went back to the station and came back here. No point in staying. And I've decided I don't want to convert anyway. I realised if I convert I can't have a pint down the Legion with the boys. And I'm not sure I'm ready to make that kind of sacrifice," said Dave.

"Quite right Dave, you have to make sure

your priorities are in order before making big life decisions," added Janice.

"Right, I'm off to 'Spoons for something to eat. I'm starving," said Dave.

"Did you not eat while you were in Cardiff? You've been gone ages."

"No, I went straight there and came straight back. I'm not into foreign food."

"It's Cardiff Dave, not Marrakech, it's hardly foreign," said Carol.

"Don't tell me you took your passport Dave?" Janice added.

"I know that, I meant the takeaway food. Either way I'm starving, so have a lovely evening, I'm off to fill my face."

5.31pm

Elsewhere a feathered friend was coming to the conclusion that no one was going to provide any more morsels to eat. And strutting round and round the fountain was proving useless. It had been a good day.

~~~
~~~

Carol and Janice watched the passengers alight, no one was getting on.

"Go on then, convince me," said Carol, out of the blue.

"Convince you of what?" replied Janice.

"I have racked my brains and noted everything, and I can't make sense of anything. And I got to thinking of your suggestion about the box of teeth as being suspicious. But I'm still not seeing how they could be involved. So, go on, convince me."

"Well, I hadn't given it too much thought, but you said there were fifty smaller boxes of false teeth in one bigger box."

"Yes," replied Carol.

"And each of them had a separate identification number on the inside lid. True?"

"Yes."

"Well, what if each one was an order for a different client. And what if they were actually being bought off the black market."

"Who buys dentures illegally?"

"Where there's money to be made, people will buy and sell anywhere and anything."

"Okay, but it can't be a case of one size fits all. Especially when you consider they are all individually labelled."

"Ah yes, I hadn't got that far. Like I said, some of the story I hadn't given too much thought to. I just had a feeling the box was suspicious. Unless you have any other ideas."

"There are things that do not make sense regarding the dentures, but I still don't think they're suspicious, just odd."

"Have you not read Agatha Christie, it's those little details that help solve the mysteries. You need to get those *'leettle grey cells'* working," said Janice in her best Belgian accent.

"Thank you Miss Marple."

"Poirot! It's Hercule Poirot that refers to his little grey cells," said Janice.

"I was always suspicious of Miss Marple. How does an old lady, totally unconnected to local law enforcement, always manage to find herself encountering so many dead people and then just happen to solve the murders? Either the local police are thick as mince, or she's framing others for her murders," said Carol.

"I've always thought the same of Mrs

Fletcher. She was always selling best sellers based on the murders she just happened to 'help' solve. Why doesn't anyone point out she's the murderer? We all know it. So I'm telling you, be careful dismissing the false teeth," warned Janice.

"I'll make a footnote if that makes you happy."

"Thank you, could you also put next to it *'Janice said this from the start'*, said Janice looking across to Carol typing the footnote into her phone.

"Anything else while I'm typing?"

"No, that's all for now," Janice said in approval.

Carol mused over her notes and fell into deep thought. Janice just zoned out, her brain had done a lot today and was long overdue a reboot.

5.39pm

Enid had long left the converted shed. She had been totally unaware she had been watched as she left and neither was the next elderly visitor any the wiser as she entered. Across the road was a woman sitting in a car noting the comings and goings. Her colleague was in charge of filming events.

Enid had made it home. The person sent to follow her sent a text of the address, waited for the response and then left the way they had came.

5.42pm

The latest train pulled into the station, waited until its passengers got off and smoothly pulled away.

A warm and steady breeze blew across the station. It had been a long but interesting day so far. It was never as interesting as this usually, so the day had flown by. Carol and Janice were always happy to stay until evening during the summer months.

"Hannah has just sent me a text, she says she has more info regarding the helmet situation," said Janice, breaking the silence.

"Go on."

"Well there's been another change. Apparently now it's a full crash helmet, you know, the ones with the visor," said Janice gesturing the visor motion with her hand.

"Yes I know what a visor is, go on, what about it?"

"Well nothing really, it's just that they've gone from bicycle helmets to full crash helmets like Lewis Hamilton. Except you wont be sponsored by some big oil company."

"Okay, who have we got instead?"

"'*Gala Bingo*' and *'Pure Cremation'.*"

"Goodness me, they definitely know their target audience."

"Hey, not bad for a mobility scooter race, whatever brings in the money, don't knock it."

"I suppose," said Carol

Janice popped her phone back in her pocket. As she did, a familiar feathered friend and his girlfriend landed on platform two. Janice didn't notice.

"Your friends are back, look," said Carol nodding in the pigeons direction.

"Where?" said Janice, turning her head left and right.

"Just there." Carol had to point directly at the two pigeons.

"Wow, how did I miss them coming back? Hello guys."

The two pigeons weren't really bothered by the attention they received from Janice. She didn't have food for them so they didn't care. And why should they. Had they known however what observations had been made about them, the discussions that had gone on and the report made, they still wouldn't have cared. They're pigeons.

Janice however was thrilled to see them back. She whipped out her phone again to write the latest sightings and observations of the two birds, she also took a couple of photos for identification. This too would be sent to the RSPB at the end of the day.

"Okay it's 5.45pm, the pigeons seem to have had a good day, still in good health." Janice was talking as she was typing.

"How do you know they're in good health? How do you know that one hasn't got a dicky heart? And that one IBS?" asked Carol.

"I don't, but I don't have the time or the

resources to take them for a medical, so my professional judgement will have to do," said Janice.

"Fair enough." Carol pulled out her phone and sent a text.

Pam read the message, Carol wanted to go back to the office and see the CCTV footage. She wrote back *'no probs, I'll tell Bill to set it up.'*

"Right I'm off back to the office with Pam, I'll be back in a bit," announced Carol to Janice.

"What for?"

"Bill is setting up the CCTV footage from earlier today, to see what we can see."

"We've been here all day. I haven't seen anything suspicious, unless you have, but I guess you would have said if you had," said Janice.

"Well you never know, we might have been in deep conversation and missed something. That and It's really going to bug me unless I see for myself. Right, see you in a bit, Pam's waiting for me."

"Okay, see you in a bit, bring me back something nice. And don't forget to keep your eyes open for any suspicious false teeth."

Carol headed off for the office. Janice pulled out her phone and sent a text.

A message was received in a surveillance car not too far away. It read, *'Do you realise there's a box of fifty sets of dentures in the lost and found at the station? Dutch writing, individually numbered. Carol has dismissed it, I reckon it's suspicious. Hope that helps. See you soon. xx.'*

Alison gave a rye smile. Janice may act daft at times but she's not stupid. And she really doesn't know how close to the mark she is. Alison responded with a thumbs up. No need to give away more information than needed, or that they have already been dusted for finger-prints.

Janice nodded, message received. Alison was giving nothing away. Which meant she must be close to the bone. Even so, Carol wouldn't be convinced, she'd say she was reading into things.

"What do you think? Am I right or am I right? Don't pretend like you don't care. I know you've been thinking about this all day. Oh! don't turn your back on me, especially after I fed you earlier. You are not going to impress your girlfriend that way."

Both pigeons just kept strutting around, oblivious they were being spoken to. They walked to the other platform.

"Oh, where are you two going? I was talking to you pair. Just when I thought we had an understanding. I'll put that in my report."

~~~

Pam pressed the code to gain access to the office. Bill had discovered a new game to play on his phone.

"How much?" The inflection in his voice rose higher as he said it.

"What's up my little munchkin?" asked Pam. Carol closed the door behind them. "Would you like a mocha this time Ca?" she said, shortening Carol's name.

"Oh yes please, that'll make a nice change. Thank you. Have you got it ready for me Bill?"

"Yes, but we're not watching the full two and half hours are we? I haven't got the time or patience for that," exclaimed Bill.
~~~

"Is it on the laptop Bill?" asked Pam raising her voice over shoulder as she prepared the coffee machine.

"Yes, all ready to go."

"Carol, if you move the mouse over the screen you'll see a speed up icon, press that a couple of times and it'll speed up the footage. Just start without me. While I make the drinks, Bill, do you want another?"

"Oh not now Pam, I'll be up all night if I caffeinate myself again. I've got a bottle of fresh orange juice in the fridge, if you can pass it to me please, I'd be grateful, my bladder won't be though," said Bill, swivelling back and fore in his chair, keeping half an eye on the screens. Bill noticed Janice talking with someone. He recognised the face of the stranger but decided to say nothing.

"Goodness me, do I really look like that in real life?" Carol was watching footage of herself and Janice.

"Don't worry, the TV adds thirty pounds," said Pam supportively.

"Is that all?" said Bill, knowing he was risking his life as he said it.

"Shut it you," said Carol. "Okay we have coffee stain guy, we have Janice chatting with the trainspotters. We chat, chat, chat. Youngsters turn up. Posh dog woman. Chat, chat, chat. Pam brought us coffees. Have you killed anyone recently Pam? Robbed anyone? Or committed any other felony?"

"Not this week, sorry. Hang around and Bill might come to a rough and swift end." Pam put Carol's mocha on the desk.

"We all chat, chat, chat. Pam heads off for chips. Thanks for those by the way Bill.

"You're welcome," said Bill.

"Who is this elderly couple?" asked Pam.

"Not sure, Janice talked with them, while I was in the loo."

"Here we go," said Pam, "who's this fella?"

"Oh yes, we couldn't help notice his tattoos," said Carol.

"He's messing around with his cello quite a bit," observed Pam, "pause it."

"What's he checking for, he's spending a good amount of time checking his cello. Unless there's no cello in it."

"Ooo, that's a point. Is this the only camera angle Bill?" asked Pam.

Bill looked over to the laptop, "Yep, only one camera on that area."

"I bet you that's our man," said Carol confidently.

""What do you mean *your man*'? How do you know he's who you are looking for?" asked Bill.

"Well in the time frame we've been given, he's the only one acting shifty. Who carries an empty cello case around?" said Carol.

"That's a bit of a leap isn't it. You can't actually see it's empty, he may actually just be checking his cello," said Bill, "you are getting a bit carried away if you ask me."

"We should let Alison know," said Carol.

"Don't get me involved," said Bill, "If you say you've gone through the footage, she'll know I've shown it to you and that we are all in cahoots together."

"Bill," said Pam firmly, "Alison isn't daft, she knows Carol won't let things alone. She's always one step ahead, that, and she knows how to push all our buttons."

"You know she's right," said Carol, "I don't like it, but she is right."

"Okay, true," said Bill. "But I still think you are barking up the wrong tree, that young guy with the cello has nothing to do with anything. I wouldn't mention anything to Alison if I was you."

"What was so expensive by the way? You weren't happy about something when we came in," asked Carol.

"Do you know they wanted £5.99 for that game and you still had to buy levels to carry on the game," replied Bill.

"Those nasty people, I'll tell them off for you," said Pam, like she was talking to a small child, "just after we have caught our criminal mastermind giving Alison the slip."

6.00pm

Alison pulled up outside the address she had been given. She told her colleague to remain in the car. She knocked on the door and waited.

Her colleague watched from the car. He saw the front door open, Alison introduced herself, the elderly woman welcomed Alison into her home, and the door closed behind her. All he could do now was wait, well almost. He fished around in his coat pocket and pulled out a large chocolate bar he hadn't long bought from the shop. Experience had taught him to always come armed and ready with supplies, you just never know when you will be called upon to sit in a car and do nothing. Community policing at its best.

He enjoyed working with Alison although it felt like working for her rather than with her. She was genuinely a nice person, but he knew she could bring the toughest of men to their knees with ease.

He wasn't really sure what they were actually doing, but he trusted Alison knew what was going on and that was good enough for him.

One thing was criminal for sure. He looked down at his 'large' chocolate bar and was sure they were getting smaller by the day. Drug dealers and petty criminals he could arrest and feel he was contributing to society. But he felt he was powerless against the shameless chocolate giants who seemed to be able to do what they wanted. Chocolate addicts everywhere, getting fleeced for every penny they had to satisfy their fix. How do these people sleep at night?

Nothing in police academy could have ever prepared him for this intense feeling of injustice.

Nevertheless if he didn't eat it soon it would be completely melted, it already felt soft.

6.15pm

Janice was still alone on the platform. She got to thinking about her school days at Glan Afan Comprehensive.

"I wonder," she pulled out her phone.

She opened up her socials and typed in Glan Afan to see what came up.

"Oh I remember that," she said, as she fell quickly into the nostalgia rabbit hole, every thought spoken out loud. "Oh look 'Bunhead', I loved her, she was great. Oh I know," Janice typed in Michael Sheen, "I wonder if I was there at the same time as our Michael." She quickly got her answer, "No is the answer. Not far off though, just one year after him. Oh I wonder if I sat in his chair."

Carol and Pam appeared on the platform and headed back to Janice.

"Did you miss us?" asked Pam.

"Absolutely, I've been sat here pining for you," said Janice. "Were you in school at the same time as Michael Sheen Carol?"

"Yes, but I don't remember him and I doubt he'll remember me. Why?" asked Carol, a little flustered all of a sudden.

"Just going through old pics of school people have posted and then I wondered if I was there at the same time as Mr Sheen, turns out I wasn't. Shall I ask him if he remembers you?"

"What? How would you do that? Umm, no, why would you do that?" asked Carol

"For fun, I'll DM him on Instagram and see if he responds," said Janice as if it was obvious.

"You'll DM him? When I was younger DM's were *Dr. Martens*, what's a DM?" asked Carol.

"They still are *Dr. Martens* but they are also a direct message to a person's social account. Sometimes famous people respond, so you never know Mr. Sheen might have noticed you in school." She started typing and asked the question.

"Well if he responds," said Pam, "tell him Carol won't be available Saturday evening but she may be available Sunday, just in case he wants to meet up and catch up on old times."

"Good point and that'll give Carol enough time to buy some decent clothes," said Janice.

"Oh, what do you mean 'decent clothes'? I have plenty of decent clothes, thank you," protested Carol.

Janice and Pam looked at each other and raised their eyebrows.

"Shut up you pair, I've got plenty of good clothes and you know it. Anyway, why am I even entertaining this fallacy? He won't remember me, he won't respond if he did, and he definitely isn't going to meet up with me. But if he does respond and wants to meet up, tell him I am actually available anytime except Saturday evening," specified Carol.

"Fair enough, I'll make sure he knows," said Janice.

"While we're doing this, can we get in touch with Denzel Washington? If he gets in touch, I am definitely available Saturday. Ain't no way

I'm spending the evening with you guys if Denzel wants to do dinner," said Pam.

"You didn't go to school with Denzel," protested Carol.

"So what? Aim for the stars and hope to clear the trees I say."

"Right, that's sent to Michael. I put a small kiss kiss on the end. So what did you guys spot on the CCTV?" asked Janice.

"Lots of us talking. But we did find something really interesting. Do you remember the cellist with the tattoos?" asked Carol.

"Yes, what about him?"

"Well he spent a lot of time checking inside his cello case. I don't believe he had a cello in there. I reckon he was checking something else."

"Checking what?" asked Janice.

"I don't know, I haven't got that far yet," said Carol.

"Bill says Carol is barking up the wrong tree and she's getting too excited about the whole affair," said Pam.

"I agree," said Janice, "just let Alison tell us on Saturday what's been happening." Janice finished typing on her phone. "And that's the second message sent."

"You've really sent a message to Denzel?" asked Pam with a hint of excitement.

"No. Not exactly," said Janice with the tiniest of smiles.

"What do you mean 'not exactly'? asked Pam.

"I've sent it to Rob Brydon instead," said Janice, now laughing.

"What?! Rob Brydon?" exclaimed Pam in shock.

"Aim for stars I say," added Carol with a rye smile.

"I've sent him your availability too," said Janice.

"You idiot. I'm going out Saturday and I don't know when I'm free next," said Pam, "after I've been supplying you guys with drinks and chips all day."

"He's probably busy anyway, so don't worry too much about it," said Carol.

"So there was nothing or no one else on the footage then?" asked Janice.

"There was the odd person, that elderly couple that you spoke to, other than that, nothing else you could consider to be suspicious," said Carol.

6.39pm

Elsewhere, an officer was still waiting in an unmarked car. The chocolate had been wolfed down. He still couldn't believe they put 'large' on the packaging. Medium size, yes, large, no chance. Surely there must be some sort of regulatory body to complain to. He was sure chocolate bars were smaller than when he was a child. He googled for the actual weight discrepancies. It didn't take too long to find the information he needed for evidence to support his case. Police training had taught him well. However the evidence wasn't so straightforward. Kitkat is 29% bigger? What? Okay, some were definitely smaller though. Hmmm this would be harder to prove than first thought. He gave it further thought.

The front door opened once again. This time Alison exited like she was one of the family. She was given a huge hug before being allowed to leave. Alison waved goodbye as she returned to the car.

Her colleague put his phone away. He watched Alison come towards the car and open the door. She sat down and closed the door. "Well that was nice, let's go," said Alison. He didn't expect her to offer any more information and he didn't ask for any. "Back to the office," she added.

6.41pm

Elsewhere, Jack turned off the lights to his converted shed as his elderly assistant Eunice, made her way back to the house. He bolted the shed door and snapped shut the padlock. He pulled out his smartphone and opened the security app and alarmed the shed.

"Have we missed 'Pointless'?" he asked.

"Ages ago. What do you want for tea?" asked Eunice.

"Can we have pie and chips with that thick gravy you do?"

"I'll have to check if we have enough," she replied as she looked to see what her husband was up to. "Where have you gone?" she didn't have to wait long to find out.

From inside the outside toilet she could hear where he was.

"Sorry, I needed to go again. You go in, I'll come in, in a moment."

"Unbelievable," she responded, opening the back door, "you could at least shut the toilet door behind you, not everyone wants to see you do that."

"I beg to differ."

6.44pm

Meanwhile on the platform Pam had returned to helping Phil clean and do a security check. Carol and Janice remained seated.

"Oh look at that," said Janice excitedly, pointing at the tracks.

"Look at what?" asked Carol, a little startled by the sudden excitement.

"There, on the other side of the track. A grass snake making its way down the side of the track. I wouldn't have thought you'd see one of those down here."

"It must be lost," said Carol, "ask if it's lost."

"Are grass snakes poisonous?" asked Janice.

"Few snakes are poisonous, so no. But if you mean venomous, still no. Adders are the only ones that are venomous around here."

"What do grass snakes do to protect themselves?" asked Janice.

"They will pretend to be dead or if you touch them they empty their anus on you and you'll stink for ages."

"Great. That's brilliant, millions of snakes around the world, like cobras, pythons, rattlesnakes, all will kill you if you touch them, to defend themselves. But here in Wales they poo on you. Did we teach them that or did they work that out for themselves?" asked Janice.

"Do you want to name him or her before it leaves?" asked Carol as they watched the snake slither away.

"Kelly Jones. I don't know why, but it just seems right." answered Janice.

"Kelly Jones will be happy," said Carol.

"He'll write a song about it and it'll make him millions."

"I'm sure he's not that desperate for material just yet."

"He could sing about the 'green green grass snake of home'," suggested Janice, "a tribute to Sir Tom."

"Have you ever thought of being a ghost-writer for artists? You seem to have a natural talent right there. Finish off the song and send it to Kelly Jones," suggested Carol.

"Yes! And I will also earn royalties from it, for the rest of my life, I will never need to work again."

"You don't need to work anyway, so it won't make a difference. But you would have the satisfaction of writing a song for one of our Welsh treasures."

"That is a very lovely thought, I'll make some notes."

6.49pm

The next train pulled into the station.

"Carol," said Janice

"What?" Carol was scrolling through her phone.

"Carol," Janice was trying to be earnest while keeping her voice fairly low.

"What?" said Carol, a little more irritated this time.

"Look!"

"At what?"

"The guy with the tattoos is back," said Janice.

"Seriously? Where?" said Carol looking round. "Oh, he is too." She immediately texted Pam. *'Pam, pretend to do a security check on the guy with the cello and tattoos'.*

'What am I checking for?' came the reply.

'Check he's got a cello first and then look for anything suspicious'. Carol wrote with urgency.

Pam walked calmly down the platform and approached the unsuspecting young man.

Carol also got up, and she too walked towards the young man, trying to do so in a nonchalant manner. Edging ever closer.

Janice watched in amazement.

"Hello, excuse me sir," said Pam.

The young man looked up from his phone, "Hello."

"Hello sir, my name is Pam and I'm station

staff, I need to do a security check on your luggage, if that's ok? It's a routine random spot check we need to do. Would it be okay to open the cello case please?"

"Umm, certainly." He said opening the case up without hesitation. He looked up and was suddenly aware of another woman staring to see inside his case."

"Please don't mind my colleague." said Pam, who gave a look to Carol, as if to say *what on earth are you doing?*

~~~

Bill could see everything clearly from his chair, and wondered why the poor young man had been accosted by Pinky and Perky.

"What on earth are they up to now," he said out loud leaning forward to the monitor. "That poor boy, it can't be good whatever it is." He continued watching as they made him remove the cello and then return it back to its case. He continued to watch as Carol stepped forward and was evidently going to frisk the poor guy. "Oh no!" Bill quickly got on the tannoy, "All
~~~

staff, the security risk has now passed, I repeat security risk has now passed."

~~~

Carol immediately stepped back before she could man handle the young man. Pam shot a glance at the security camera. They then both thanked their victim and allowed him to escape.

The young man moved further down the platform to wait for the next train, he was now a little on edge thanks to the security check.

"Happy now?" asked Janice, as Pam and Carol returned to her. "Did you find guns, drugs, illegal immigrants?"

"We found nothing," said Pam, "I can't believe you made me interrogate him. You didn't have to approach him neither. Good job Bill stopped you from frisking him when he did. We could have ended up in all sorts of hot water."

"Well how else was I supposed to do a security check?" protested Carol.

"She has suckered you in Pam, I told you already she's barking up the wrong tree and you
~~~

have been drawn into her theories. And intimidating the public in the process," said Janice.

"Tell me about it. If he had been involved in anything at all illegal, he would have already done it already. Look at him, he's really agitated now, poor thing," said Pam.

"Seriously, will you just sit and enjoy the evening? Stop playing Miss Marple, because it's got you nowhere, and desperation has led you to harassing the general public. We should be going soon anyway," said Janice, straight at Carol.

6.57pm

"What would you like to watch on the telly tonight?" asked Jack, "We've got The One Show, the Hairy Bikers or the News."

"The One Show, if it's boring we can switch to the Hairy Bikers," answered Eunice.

"Did you make sure the alginate was put away this time?" asked Jack.

"Yes I did, and I labelled all the impressions correctly," Eunice replied.

"I can't understand what happened to the box of dentures we had."

"I told you, you would lose them if you weren't careful. You really need to drink less on collection days. You've probably left it next to some urinal somewhere."

"I know, but you know I can't resist a good coffee shop. I really can't remember what toilets we went to that day," said Jack.

"Look, you really need to get some tablets for your problem," insisted Eunice.

"Is drinking too much coffee a problem?" asked Jack.

"It is for you, and I meant your peeing too much is a problem. I saw Jimmy the other day and he's taking tablets from the doctor for it. Even if you only took them on collection days that would be something, and I wouldn't have to wait outside men's urinals like an idiot," said Eunice.

"Okay, I'll pop to the doctors tomorrow," said Jack. "I need to add Robbie to the group messaging."

"Can we turn over to the Hairy Bikers please?

I'm not interested in male pattern baldness or Ed Balls," asked Eunice.

7.00pm

The next train from Cardiff pulled into the station. Most of the passengers were commuters returning home from work.

The young tattooed man got on the train as quickly as he could.

Pam returned to the office to collect her things and finish up for the day.

"You're right Janice, I need to forget all this detective nonsense. I've got a bit obsessed with it all. I'll get all the goss from Alison Saturday night," announced Carol, after giving it some serious thought.

"Very good, I think we need to get going ourselves soon. It's got a lot cooler now and I have a bottle of vino in the house waiting for me."

A familiar face stepped off the train. This morning's business man had returned.

"There's your friend, the Milkybar Kid's mate, if you hurry you can quiz him about drug cartels and why he's stressed all the time," said Carol.

"Where?" asked Janice looking around. "Oh yes, he looks a lot calmer now, with his coffee in hand. He's almost got a spring in his step."

"Well?" asked Carol.

"Well what?"

"Well, are you going to speak to him?" asked Carol.

"Oh no, I think I'd like to keep the mystery going. It's probably for the best. And he's probably thinking the same. He's probably got this undying urge to speak to me too, but can't bring himself to approach me," said Janice, "something that affects most men.

"You're probably right, but he seems to do a convincing act of not being aware you exist, let alone resist any urge to approach you to speak to you," added Carol.

"Okay, no need to bring reality into the picture. Come on, let's pack up."

They both got their things together and got up to leave.

"I've enjoyed today," said Janice walking towards the steps.

"Yes, it's been nice, busier than usual, but nice," replied Carol, "what happened to your pigeons in the end?" she asked as they ascended the exit stairs.

"While you were harassing the tattooed guy, I noticed them fly up underneath the shelter. They perched themselves on one of the ledges. I doubt they've gone to bed, it's a bit early and light for that. I'd imagine they are winding down for the evening, after a busy day foraging," said Janice, "I'm not keen enough to hang around to find out what they will be getting up to."

"Are you going to do a follow up report to the RSPB?" asked Carol.

"Of course, it could be of national ornithological interest. Kate Humble will be ringing me up for an interview soon, for one of those Countryfile programmes," replied Janice, as if stating the obvious, "I will use poetic licence to describe how they end their day."

"Make it up you mean. Well, keep your phone charged, you never know," said Carol.

They both started making their way down the stairs on the other side, and out the exit.

The evening breeze was much stronger now. It would die down in an hour or so.

Carol yawned as they made their way back home, retracing their steps.

As they left the station, coming the other way, towards the station, Carol and Janice were passed by two police officers. One tall male and the other a medium height female.

"Hi Janice," said the female officer as they passed.

"Hi Kath," replied Janice, "don't let Alison work you too hard."

"I won't, not that we have a choice. Have a lovely evening," said Kath. The two officers continued their conversation.

"What's happening? Do you know something I don't?" asked Carol, with a slight tone of frustration.

"I just said hello, you really need to learn to let things go," said Janice with a rye smile. A knowing smile that would only wind her sister up. It didn't matter whether she did know something or not, the aim was solely to give the impression she did. Sending Carol's brain into a spin.

"You do know something! You are just not saying. Why are the police going to the train station? What have you not told me?"

Carol had bitten, Janice didn't flinch and carried on walking home.

"I don't know any more than I've already told you," said Janice honestly. "They are probably just going to show face, to give a presence. So everyone feels safer. We can go back and ask Kath if you like?" Janice was thoroughly enjoying herself. Not knowing something juicy was Carol's kryptonite.

"No that's fine," said Carol reluctantly, fighting the urge to do just that, go back and ask Kath. She chose to walk on, although in silence.

Janice knew the silence on the outside, meant inside Carol's head her mind was screaming.

"I don't want chips tonight after all. Since we had some already. Do you fancy an Indian?" asked Janice.

Carol was still deep in thought. "Umm, yes that sounds nice."

They headed back up Oakwood Street. "That BMW has gone, I bet you the police took it away after they arrested that woman this morning," said Janice.

"Maybe. I'm ready for a glass of wine now, my head is shot. I can't think no more," replied Carol.

They both continued up the street. As they went, behind them a police car and an un-marked police car pulled up outside a house. Alison waited until Carol and Janice had almost made it to their street, before getting out of the unmarked car. "You stay here," she said to the driver. He remained obediently.

7.15pm

"I think they've lost weight," said Eunice.

"Who?" asked Jack.

"Who do you think? The Hairy Bikers. They both were quite chunky. They look like they've shed a pie or two. Which is impressive in itself considering how much they eat. I'd end up the same if I used that much butter every day."

"You could still pass as a Hairy Biker though."

"Shut your face, I'm not that hairy."

Suddenly there was a ring of a doorbell.

"Did you book anyone in for tonight Jack?" asked Eunice, getting out of her chair to open the door.

"No, I wasn't expecting anyone."

Eunice walked down the hallway and could see a figure through the glass, she opened the door to her visitor.

"Hello Eunice."

"Oh, hello Alison," replied Eunice.

7.18pm

Carol opened the gate she had shut this morning. The windows were gleaming after the window cleaner had been. She turned the key and opened the front door.

"Where's that wine?" said Carol loudly as she entered the hallway and made her way through to the kitchen.

"Let's order food first," Janice shouted through as she closed the door behind her. "How are you feeling now?"

"What do you mean?"

"Well, how do you feel now? You know, after not solving the case."

"What case? You guys were right, I was barking up the wrong tree," said Carol looking for the corkscrew.

"I think Alison was pushing your buttons. She does it on purpose to wind you up."

"Why though? Why would she do that to me?"

"She knows you can take it. She does her job with her eyes shut, it's too easy for someone like her, she needs something else to stimulate her. You should see it as a compliment and her way of showing you affection," said Janice.

Carol was forced to concede her little sister was right.

Janice flicked the television on, "Oh, it's the Hairy Bikers again, I'm sure they've lost weight," she said, at the same time she opened the drawer to the side cabinet and pulled out a menu to order the takeaway Indian. She could use the app on her phone, but she felt there was something nice about having a real menu in her hands and making a phone call to make the order.

"What do you want from the Indian?" she shouted to Carol.

"The usual please, chicken korma with keema naan, please."

"Do you not want to try something a bit more exciting?"

"I've never done exciting and I am not starting now. Boring, please."

"Boring it is," said Janice to herself. At the same moment Carol popped the cork of the wine bottle.

7.21pm

Alison was now sitting in the living room with Eunice and Jack. Two officers were at the inside of the front door.

"Go on then, how did you know?" asked Eunice. Eunice and Jack made no pretence. There was no point trying to bluff Alison, they knew they had been caught. It had been like a twisted version of cat and mouse and they were both staring at the cat.

"Let's just say we've been watching you for a while," said Alison. "I'm actually quite sad it's over, I was enjoying the sport. It's nice to be pitted against a couple of high level players. I must admit this was one of your best schemes yet, I look forward to the next one," she said, smiling warmly.

"That's very kind of you to say so love," said Jack. "Would you like a cuppa?"

"No thanks Jack, not while I'm on duty," replied Alison, "I'm supposed to be interrogating you right now."

"Fair enough, when we leave I'll make it seem like we've been roughed up," said Jack, helpfully.

"Thanks Jack, you're a sweetie."

"Did you find the box we lost?" asked Jack.

"We did. You left it outside the men's toilets at the station."

Eunice slapped Jack on the leg. "You and your weak tiny bladder."

Jack winced, "Ow, careful, you'll set my bladder off again."

"We managed to lift some prints off the box in the lost and found at the station. We were hoping you were going to go back for it and catch you with the goods, but that wasn't to be," said Alison. "It's quite a scheme. Getting

Drug-dealer Dave involved as a red herring, that was a nice touch."

"Well I would like to take credit for that but he sort of got himself involved," said Eunice.

"What do you mean?" asked Alison, confused, as she thought she had had it all worked out.

"As you probably already know the girl you arrested in the BMW was meant to be collecting an order to take back to Wolverhampton with her. Some weeks ago, all was well, she got down here safely, parked up where we told her too and at the correct time. The order was ready and packed at our front door. What we didn't account for was Dave taking a shine to her as he passed the car. He got chatting to her and decided to sit with her in the car, thinking things were going really well. So when he saw her today, as she was waiting for us to return, to collect the next batch of teeth, he must have thought it was a second date. He's such a plonker that boy!"

"Oh I see," said Alison. "That's a shame. If it makes you feel any better, he wasn't too much of a distraction for us. Once we had your prints, we were just waiting to see if anyone else was involved. How big was the operation in the end?" she knew she could ask this and get a straight answer as this wasn't the first time they had gone through this.

The way it usually worked was, Eunice and Jack would think up an ingenious black market scheme, this would run for some time, sometimes years, eventually there would be a leak somewhere. Alison would be asked to investigate, she would eventually get evidence that would lead her to Eunice and Jack. They would do some time in prison, get let out early with good behaviour and the whole process would start again. Only as they got older, there were fewer guns and mafia tactics and more pettier crimes and shorter stints behind bars. This latest scheme had been their best for a while.

"You know about Wolverhampton. So we had clients from Edinburgh, London, Bristol, most of South Wales and across Devon and Cornwall. We even had some celebrities ask for sets of dentures," said Eunice with a sense of pride.

"Really? Like who?" asked Alison with real surprise.

"Bob Mortimer," chimed in Jack, "We had Dec from 'Ant n Dec' and Susan Boyle."

"But you mustn't say anything Al. I'll tell you anything else you need to know, but keep our celebs out of it please. Getting us arrested must have got you promoted a few times over the years," said Eunice. This time it was Alison's turn to read between the lines. Eunice had a lot of dirt on Alison and hadn't had to play any of those cards as of yet. They both knew this was a game of cat and mouse, and they both played it very well.

"Mums the word, I will reveal only what I need to. Hopefully, you'll only get a few months for this one. Can I tell the gang about the celebs?" Alison asked.

"Janice and Carol? Of course, but don't reveal that I already know who they are, I played dumb this afternoon," Eunice said with a smile.

"I won't, but I have a funny suspicion they may have been doing the same."

All of sudden, a familiar snoring noise came from the armchair. Eunice and Alison turned to see Jack slumped to one side, lip drooping and saliva escaping the side of his mouth.

"Well that's a first, I've never had someone fall asleep as they were getting arrested. Come on, is there anything you need to bring with you? Since this is a working relationship I promise not to cuff you both this time," Alison said smiling.

She called the officers from the front door to escort Eunice and Jack to the car, before heading to the police station for processing. At the same time she pulled out her phone and sent a text to a local journalist she had saved on her phone.

'You can go ahead with the story, I've made two arrests, they will remain anonymous, probably further arrests to be made following further investigation, you didn't hear that from me'

Alison made up that last bit, she knew Eunice and Jack were at the heart of the operations. If the courts got the impression from a news report that they were just pawns in a bigger operation and if this resulted in a shorter sentence for Eunice and Jack, who was she to get involved and correct them.

7.35pm

Janice had ordered the Indian takeaway from the menu she had studied to death and eventually settled upon the same thing she has every time.

She slumped into the sofa and laid her head back, closing her eyes. The noise of the shower running upstairs was the only noise she could hear.

It had been a strange old day, it was almost never that exciting sitting at the station. Everything and nothing happened. There seemed to be a lot of activity, separate incidents, Alison appearing and disappearing, lots of questions and no conclusions. Which now left her brain in a spin, especially after it had been a particularly warm day. She wasn't sure she could wait until Saturday to get the full story from Alison. She could feel her eyes getting heavy.

7.37pm

Carol switched off the shower. She was still trying to piece the events of the day together but nothing was fitting into place. This was getting silly now, she only went to the station to sit and people watch. She wasn't prepared for this amount of cerebral activity at the end of the day. Enough was enough, *'come on, switch off,'* she said to herself, *'we've got an Indian on the way and a bottle of red waiting downstairs.'*

She grabbed her towel and headed to her bedroom to get herself dressed.

7.38pm

Pam had decided she had had enough for the day. She said her goodbyes to Bill and left to meet her husband waiting for her in the car.

She pulled the car door shut and had the usual catch up with her husband. Soon while her husband was having a rant about the 'boys at work', she stared out the window and had a rye smile as she thought about her day with the girls. It was never dull with those two, well sometimes it is, but today wasn't one of the days. It was definitely one that will be talked about for a while.

7.41pm

Janice awoke suddenly, "What? Where am I?" and then saw Carol with the takeaway.

"Come on, let's dish up."

"Oh good," said Janice, coming round quickly.

She got off the sofa, leaving the TV on. The evening news streamed into the now empty room. Not that it could be heard from the kitchen.

While Carol and Janice poured themselves glasses of wine in the kitchen and sorted out who was having what, the main headlines ended and the local news began.

"I wonder what really happened today," said Janice, taking a bite of her onion bhaji.

"Something happened, I've tried to stop thinking about it. I'm going to drink my wine and eat my food, and try to find a boxset to binge on for the evening," said Carol.

"How's about a film instead?" offered Janice.

8.21pm

In the living room the local news was still streaming through.

"And tonight in still developing news, a report

from Port Talbot says an underworld syndicate of black market dental traders was disrupted today after two dangerous gang members were arrested at their home by police in an undercover sting operation.

It is reported over £2000 pounds worth of imported dentures made to order, were recovered from Port Talbot Parkway station after they were left there by mistake. Although it seems some of the goods had already been taken. Police say even though only two gang members were arrested, it seems the syndicate leaders are still at large. They are hoping DNA evidence will lead to more arrests."

8.22pm

Carol and Janice picked up their trays full of takeaway and wine and headed back to the living room and headed for the sofa.

"And that's the end of this evening's news, goodnight/nos da," concluded the Welsh newsreader bilingually.

"We never did catch up with this evening's news did we, to see if Mr Stresshead had reported gang operations in the area?" said Carol sitting down.

"Let's forget about that," said Janice, shovelling a forkful of curry into her mouth, "we probably haven't missed much, come on, stick a film on."

8.23pm

THE END